Cinder Rabbit

Volume 1 of
The
Saddlebag Chronicles

Brock Hunt

This book is a work of fiction. All characters and events portrayed are the product of the author's imagination or are used fictitiously. All rights are reserved. No parts of this book may be reproduced in any form or by any means without the prior written permission of the publisher, except for brief quotations used in connection with reviews.

Published under the supervision of
Scotchwood Hill Publishing Service
3101 Scotchwood Drive
Jonesboro, Arkansas 72405

ISBN: 978-1-969292-01-9

"And now that you don't
have to be perfect, you can be
good."

John Steinbeck

ACKNOWLEDGMENTS

To Jesus my savior, and all the teachers who encouraged me. To my family who took me to church and made me feel welcome. To everyone who helped me in the journey it took to get here. To Martha Rodriguez and Patrica Blake for their assistance in formatting and editing. To Writers Ink and the Current River Writers for their friendship and knowledge. To Rainy Louis for the beautiful cover art.

CONTENTS

Chapter One

Genesis

At the ripe age of twelve, Riley had only come to the library for some peace and quiet and to get away from the constant fighting that defined his parents' marriage. They never fought about anything understandable or anything that could be resolved, such as money, schedules, or any triggering event. The boy believed their father was bored if he wasn't yelling about something, and their mother confused drama with happiness.

Today was no different. Their parents were fighting and poorly trying to hide the fact. Olivia locked herself in her room. She was doing whatever she could to drown them out. The eight-year-old's soul already had far too many miles on it.

The children had learned to stay away when that happened. When they tried to intervene, they'd be called out for the worthless, ungrateful, good-for-nothings their parents called them. Riley had thought that once his sister was born, things would be better. He was wrong. How naive his five-year-old mind had been.

Now, he aimlessly perused the walls of books surrounding him, hoping to find a hidden treasure. Betty, the ancient white-haired librarian, was asleep at the counter with her mouth agape and *War and Peace* resting on her lap. Riley found the latch almost by mistake.

"This wall is load bearing," Riley whispered to himself as he checked both sides of the white concrete wall. The wall had taken up space in an already crammed library. The building remedied the problem by placing two bookshelves on each side of it. However, the wall itself was only about as wide as he was. He returned to the latch he had found and pushed the shelf out of the way once more. This revealed a dark corridor, and when he stuck his hand through, he couldn't feel the other side of the wall. Riley hadn't been looking for this, but now an adventure presented itself to him.

"Nothing ventured, nothing gained," he said as he crossed the threshold.

He had expected to find some stairs that would lead him up or down. Instead, he found a long corridor that seemed to stretch farther than the library itself. Gazing forward, he saw a bright light coming from an illuminated room. He started toward it when a figure appeared to step from the light. It walked on all fours and looked to Riley like a large German shepherd. The creature noticed Riley and started toward him. Riley considered turning back, but the beast was already upon him. Right before the figure could lunge at him, it reared back on its hind legs and placed its front paws on Riley's shoulders.

"Welcome, my boy!" the figure exclaimed.

To say Riley was shocked was a gross understatement. He was completely floored by the creature in front of him. What he had thought to be a German shepherd was undeniably a wolf. The sharp features of his nose, muzzle, and ears displayed a wild quality lost on their domestic counterparts. Even hunched, he was a good head taller than Riley. The paws on his shoulders were a mix of human hands and canine pads.

The things that drew Riley's attention were his eyes and smile. The eyes were large with a shimmering gold that stood out against the wolf's tan fur. The smile, despite revealing sharp teeth and black brims, radiated the warmth of seeing an old family member.

"Hhh…. Hi," Riley stammered, not knowing what else to say.

"Sorry if I startled you," the wolf said, withdrawing his paws. "It's just been so long since I've had a guest."

The wolf turned back toward the light and said, "Come in and let me show you around." With his tail wagging behind him, he began leading Riley toward the end of the hall.

Riley followed, still in stunned silence at the beast in front of him.

Before reaching the illuminated room, the wolf turned back to face him.

"I am so sorry. I forgot to introduce myself." He reached out one of his paws, "I'm Saddlebags."

Riley reached out and shook the wolf's paw. "RR…Riley," he stammered.

"Well, Riley." Saddlebags stepped into the threshold and pushed open the door. "Welcome to my library."

Chapter 2

The Wolf in the Tan Sweater

Crossing the threshold, Riley's eyes lit up in amazement. Standing before him was a tremendous library that stretched in all directions beyond what he could see. Bookcases, standing as tall as trees, were stuffed with books of all kinds. Riley looked up and could see the night sky…. no wait, the sun was shining through a skylight…. or both? Looking closer, the night sky condensed itself along the ceiling of the library and acted as shades for the natural skylights. The night sky was complete with twinkling stars and a full moon that seemed to rest on the clouds.

"You like that?" Saddlebags noticed Riley staring up at the ceiling. "That is our twilight. The sky keeps the sun's glare out of your eyes and the heat off your back. When the sun goes down, the moon and stars glow brighter. That way, it is always the perfect time for reading." He smiled as he continued to lead Riley through the library.

Riley alternated between taking in his surroundings and focusing on details. The bookcases each stood about five feet apart. The books were titled in English, Han Chinese, Hindi, Arabic, French, Spanish, Russian, and other languages that Riley did not recognize. Glancing between the shelves, he saw books float and rearrange themselves on neighboring bookshelves. Others flew past him, far above his head.

Saddlebags gestured all around him. "This library contains all the stories known to man and quite a few that aren't. Our collection grows minute by minute as young new authors add their voices and ancient stories are rediscovered.

As they continued walking, Riley glanced down a row of bookshelves and saw a small fox, walking on all fours, carrying a book in its mouth. In the next aisle, he saw two more foxes rearranging a near empty shelf with three giant stacks of books beside them.

"Who are they?" Riley asked.

"Spirits," Saddlebags answered. "They're a particular breed that collect knowledge from the everywhere of everywheres. Then, they bring and arrange it here. A young breed, too, since none of them can talk yet."

"Why not?" Riley asked.

"Well, they come from nothing. No flesh or blood like you and me. It takes them a while to build themselves up."

"How do they do that?" Riley questioned.

"Working for me is one," Saddlebags stated. "Gathering knowledge, experience, learning how things work, and helping them mature. A faster way is bonding with a person, but they're not ready for that. They still need to grow a little and learn how to talk. Besides," Saddlebags puffed up his chest, "they know I'm the boss."

It was then that Riley noticed Saddlebags was wearing a tan sweater that matched his fur.

"Nice sweater," Riley said. "Is that wool?"

"Cotton actually. My wife made it for me." He turned to me with the kindest, brightest smile Riley had ever seen. "I could ask her to make you one if you wanted."

"No, thank you," Riley said quickly.

Chapter 3

The Reading Corner

They finally turned a corner and entered a makeshift den. Nestled between two bookcases were a group of seats surrounding a fireplace. The fireplace itself crackled with a freshly made fire and seemed to have a chimney. Tables were placed on each side of overstuffed chairs. There was a couch with a bean bag chair at its foot. Saddlebags gravitated toward a rocking chair that looked both ancient and sleek and new, not to mention extremely comfortable. Riley was drawn to the blue overstuffed armchair. Upon sitting, he realized the chair had a pullout footstool.

Riley glanced over at the fireplace. "Is it safe to have a fireplace in the middle of a library?" he questioned.

"Everything in this library is protected from anything that could harm it, whether that be you or the books," Saddlebags answered. "In addition, the fire is not real, at least not in the way you think."

"That makes sense," Riley stated. The area did seem to be both darker and brighter than the surrounding library.

Just then, a trolley overflowing with refreshments was wheeled into the little nook. The top had two serving towers. One was loaded with finger sandwiches and the other with cookies, tarts, scones, and mini cakes. A ceramic floral teapot sat in the middle of them, steam lofting from the spout. The middle section held three trays. The first held an assortment of crackers, surrounding a collection of meats and cheeses. The second provided sliced apples, bananas, grapes, carrots, celery, and strawberries, which were surrounded by bowls of peanut butter and caramel dip. The third tray presented bite-sized chocolates, each decorated differently. Separating the second and third trays was a row of chocolate dipped strawberries. An assortment of candies hung off the four corners, each carrying taffy, lollipops, licorice, and other things Riley had never seen. The cart was driven by a full-grown red fox vixen wearing a faded red cardigan.

"Can I get you darlings anything?" she offered.

Saddlebags dropped his head low and loudly whispered, "Riley, who is that incredibly foxy lady?"

The fox lady rolled her eyes in a smile. "I bet you say that to all the pretty girls."

"Well, since you're the prettiest, you'll just have to be the first and last girl I talk to." Saddlebags replied.

"I better be!" the fox lady gave him a flirtatious grin.

"Your wife's not gonna like it if she hears you've been flirting with another girl!" Riley whispered harshly to him.

Saddlebags cocked his head and gave Riley a knowing smile.

After a second, Riley facepalmed and exclaimed, "She's your wife!"

"Yeah, she is." Saddlebags nodded his head.

"Well, she is beautiful," Riley said. Enchanting might have been the better word.

"Isn't she?" Saddlebags said with a contented sigh.

"Can I get you fawners anything? Or is my presence enough?" the fox lady said with a sardonic tone and a sly smile.

"Tea with honey, lemon, ginseng green and a few of those strawberries, please. Thank you, dear," Saddlebags said.

"So, the usual," the vixen replied. She turned to Riley. "Anything for you darling?"

"No, thank you," Riley shook his head.

"Are you sure? We have sodas or juice if you would like some," the vixen offered.

"I'll just have whatever Saddlebags has," Riley answered. "And some of those chocolates."

"You should know, Riley," Saddlebags spoke up, "that green tea is an acquired taste."

"Then I'll start acquiring it," Riley responded.

Saddlebags smiled at them, and then addressed his wife, "I like this pup."

"I don't know." The vixen poured Riley a cup of tea and handed him a small plate of assorted chocolates. "He looks more like a kit."

"Thank you," Riley said taking the refreshments.

"Would you like anything else, darling?" the vixen offered. "I can get you a sandwich or some soup if you would like."

"No, thank you," Riley responded.

"There's extra blankets and pillows in the table next to you if you get cold," the vixen stated.

"I'll be fine, really," Riley assured her.

"Well, if you darlings need anything just holler," she turned and walked back to her cart. "And welcome to the Haven House."

"I thought this was a library." Riley asked.

"Same difference," Saddlebags stated. "Places like this will always be a haven for weary souls and curious minds."

"Well, thanks again, Mrs...." Riley hung on.

"Call me Brooklyn," the vixen replied.

"Mrs. Brooklyn, thank you for everything, ma'am," Riley stated.

"I'm starting to like this one too." Brooklyn addressed her husband before taking the cart away.

Saddlebags slapped his knees —were they knees?— and stood up.

"Let's get down to it. What do you like?" He started pulling books from the shelf. "You strike me as a Tolkien man, perhaps C.S. Lewis, or Carrol perhaps?"

They all sounded great but.... "I was actually wondering about the ones not known to man, the ones you mentioned earlier."

It didn't seem possible, but Saddlebags smiled brighter. "I was hoping you'd say that." He placed the books back and walked to a different side of the shelf.

"These," he pointed to a shelf encased in glass, "are my family books."

"Photo albums?" Riley asked.

"This was before photos existed," He pulled out a key to unlock the album. "My family were forest guards. They protected the forest and everyone in it. The forest by its nature is full of stories." He opened the case and pulled out the first book. "These were passed down from generations of my pack until I wrote them down."

He walked over and sat in his chair. He carried two old books with him. One looked to be an old teal journal that had faded to gray with age. The other was sapphire blue with light gold lettering that Riley couldn't make out. Saddlebags held up the gray book.

"This book chronicles the life of the first Saddlebags. Because of him, the forest stories live on." He held up the sapphire one, "This is the first of many stories written by him. Which would you like to read first?"

Riley thought for a second. "I guess the book that answers the why of it all first," he responded. "Might give me a little context."

"Well then," Saddlebags cracked open the journal, "let's get started."

Chapter 4

Saddlebags: The First Chronicle

There once was a hunter who lived in the woods. He wore a multitude of animal pelts sewn together. Whenever people saw him, they wondered where he came from and where he was going. He didn't have a house or home that anybody knew about. The only things the man seemed to own were the bags he carried on his back. He had no horse or steed. The only name he allowed anyone to call him was Saddlebags.

His golden eyes had a solemn strength to them that prevented most people from calling him feral. His voice carried power in a rich timbre, but he only spoke softly and scarcely. The most anyone heard from him was a please and thank you to the traders and a polite nod to anyone who offered him a kind word.

His conversations were limited to the creatures of the woods. He would walk, and the creatures would walk with him. He would drink from the clear streams, and the creatures drank with him. He would run with the deer in the summer and the wolves in the winter. He picked berries that bloomed in the spring and gathered nuts when they fell in the autumn. He could enter all manners of dens and be welcomed as kin returning.

In the evenings, he would curl up in his dugout under the sequoia tree, and the creatures would gather around him. Raccoons, possums, beavers, squirrels, and all other furry creatures would huddle at his sides. River otters would nestle themselves under his arms. The mother rabbit would couch herself in his lap. The mountain fox would take his place on the hunter's shoulders, comforting the man's head. Moles and hedgehogs huddled at his feet. Birds of all feathers gathered in the trees overhead. Wolves and deer stood side by side, guarding the group that gathered as the new Eden.

The creatures told their stories, and Saddlebags listened.

Saddlebags closed the book. Riley hunched forward and looked puzzled. "That's it?"

"The original Saddlebags liked his solitude and didn't like talking about himself," Saddlebags explained. "This was his story as he felt fit to tell it."

"Seems short," Riley observed.

"This is just the preface," Saddlebags stated. "And he didn't write it."

"I thought the original Saddlebags wrote all the stories?" Riley queried.

"God's creatures told the stories, and all he did was listen and pass them down," Saddlebags clarified. "I was the one who finally chronicled them onto pages. These books are the summation of all the accounts the animals gave him." He looked back at the bookshelf.

"It wasn't easy. Most were either off handed, afterthoughts, or centered around themselves."

"Seems less than mindful," Riley said.

Saddlebags shrugged his shoulders. "Nobody notices a support beam until it stops working."

Riley looked down at the chocolate smeared on his fingers. "How do I...," he began.

"Tablecloth on your right," Saddlebags pulled out his own to wipe berry juice off his claws.

Riley took the cloth and wiped the chocolate from his fingers. His fingers came away spotless, while the cloth now sported chocolate stains.

"Now do this," Saddlebags grabbed an end and whipped it in the air. Riley copied him. The cloth cleared itself of any stains, as if they were never there. Riley turned the now clean cloth over and over with his hands.

"That is very cool," Riley mused.

"Of all the things you've seen, that impresses you?" Saddlebags raised an eyebrow at him.

"It's the first thing I've done," Riley replied.

"Fair enough," Saddlebags said, "I'm also obligated to mention that while the books and furniture are immune to all crumbs, chocolate smudges, and tea stains, cleaning up after oneself is polite and expected." He shot Riley a stern look.

"Yes, sir," Riley responded.

"Good," Saddlebags stated. "Now, which book shall we explore next?"

Riley scanned the glass bookcase. The volumes were leather-bound and worn with age. Faded marks seemed to denote one book from another, though Riley couldn't tell the difference between them.

"Let's just start with the first one," Riley decided.

"Excellent choice," Saddlebags pulled out the first volume from the collection, the sapphire book with the faded gold lettering.

He settled back into his chair. "This may seem familiar, but I assure you this is the first one."

Riley leaned forward in anticipation.

Chapter 5

Cinder Rabbit

There once was a fox with golden hazel eyes and dark red fur. He walked solemnly to the edge of the creek with his head held low. The fox raised his head and sniffed the air. There was no mistake. The wind carried the tinge of crisp cool air that always preceded the harsh winter. While the weather now seemed mild, the fox knew within a week the winter would come suddenly and bury all life under its harsh grasp.

The other foxes knew of this time, too. That is why tonight would be the start of the Fire Festival. In the seven days before winter gripped the land, foxes of all shapes, sizes, and colors would gather atop one of the highest mountain peaks from the far corners of the forests. There would be tremendous bonfires, various food and drinks, and the playing of the sweetest melodies. There the foxes would eat, sing, and dance until they were all full and exhausted, allowing them all to sleep soundly until the sun warmed the land once more.

The fox with the golden hazel eyes was downbeat, since he would not be attending, not that anything was truly keeping him from going. He could see his family there, as well as several friends. The baked pumpkin always brought a smile to his lips, and while he didn't like bragging, he could sing and dance better than most other foxes. The fox also knew there would be several young and beautiful vixens who would want to dance with a handsome tod such as himself. This would be the last chance for any single vulpine to find someone to snuggle with and keep warm in the coming winter months, but he had no interest in this.

The fox had adjusted to being alone. While he had several friends, many who wouldn't have minded if he had stayed with them had he been a more desperate fox, the golden-eyed fox preferred his own company and prepared his den with enough food and firewood to last until next summer if he wanted. Knowing that long walks in the sun would soon no longer be an option for him, he had taken to finding patches of sun and tanning his fur until it took on a shade of light brown.

As the golden-eyed fox knelt his head down to drink, a light gray rabbit walked up beside him and began to drink as well. This startled the fox mildly, but he showed no reaction. As he observed the rabbit out of the corner of his eye, she appeared not to have noticed him. From her build, he could tell she was female, fur groomed only recently, and muscles relaxed. While her eyes were hooded, he couldn't help but notice they were a beautiful blue. He was sure they would have shined like sapphires if the sun had been shining.

"Ahem." The fox cleared his throat. Rabbits tended to run once they noticed any fox. The rabbit continued to drink as if she had not heard him. "AHEM." The fox cleared his throat a little louder.

"Do you have something in your throat?" the rabbit asked in a flat tone not bothering to look up.

The fox was taken aback, "No...," he stammered, "I just thought you'd run."

"Why would I do that?" the rabbit asked.

"Because.... I might eat you?" the fox replied, not even sure why himself at this point.

"You might," the rabbit responded, "Or I could get struck by lightning."

The fox looked up. A few clouds were blocking the sun now, but none that could produce a thunderstorm. "How do you figure?" he asked.

"Well, my entire family just died in a fire," the rabbit said plainly.

The fox was flabbergasted but said nothing as the rabbit continued. "Anyone who was not burnt alive suffocated. My family and home are gone because I went for a walk. It was like being struck by lightning in reverse, where the tragedy hits everyone but you. So, by that logic, I'm due to be struck by lightning."

The fox opened his mouth to speak before closing it. He wasn't going to argue with her. He didn't even know how.

"So, what's your plan now?" he finally asked.

"Nothing," the rabbit replied. "I just hope that whatever kills me is relatively quick and painless and happens before winter. I hear freezing to death is a tough way to go."

The fox opened his mouth and then closed it. He didn't see the point in arguing the pros and cons of freezing to death.

Lightning seemed to strike him unexpectedly as he stared at the rabbit, casually sipping water

"Come to the festival with me," the fox stated before he knew what he was saying.

The rabbit finally glanced at him. "The festival?"

"The Fire Festival," the fox clarified, "The one hosted on top of the mountain."

"I wasn't invited," the rabbit said.

"Well, I'm inviting you," the fox pleaded. "There will be music, dancing, and more food than you'll know what to do with!"

"And other foxes?" the rabbit inquired.

"Yeah…. but," the fox finally put some thought into his suggestion.

"Alright," the rabbit stated.

"Alright?" the fox asked.

"Alright, I'll come.."

The fox's face lit up. "That's great!"

"On the condition that my safety is assured, and this isn't a part of some plot or joke."

"No, not at all," the fox rapidly shook his head, which was already swirling with ideas on how to make his crazy plan work.

"Okay," the rabbit said. "When are we going?"

The fox thought for a minute. "I'll need to get a few things, but we should meet right before dusk. Do you know of Pronghorn Clearing?" the fox asked.

"Yes." the rabbit answered. "But I thought deer didn't allow other animals near the place."

"They don't if the deer are there. When they're gone, it's open."

"Alright. I guess I'll see you then," the rabbit said as she began walking away.

"See you then," the fox replied with a big smile on his face. He was putting a proper plan together in his head, while the rabbit wore a puzzled look on her face.

Chapter 6

Firepit Prep

The rabbit later found the fox in the clearing. The trees circling the clearing had most of their bark stripped by deer antlers. The fox was stoking a small fire that gave off a sweet aroma. Next to him lay a gunny sack.

Heart beating out of her chest, the rabbit approached. "It smells good," she said, hiding a lump in her throat.

"That's the point," the fox shot her a quick glance.

"Maple?" she asked.

"Cedar," he corrected. "We want you to smell pleasant, not tasty."

The rabbit bit back her response. When the wood had burnt to ash, the fox pulled out a jug and doused the flames. He then reached into the sack and pulled out a dark red ribbon.

"Use this to tie your ears down." The fox handed her the ribbon. The rabbit did as she was instructed and fastened her ears into a ponytail. The fox then took the ashes from the fire and applied them to the crown of her head and the base of her ears.

"You're going to be shorter than most everybody at the festival. This is where they are going to smell you the most." The fox began to apply some to the base of her neck. Their eyes met.

"In case people get too close," the fox reasoned.

"Okay," the rabbit breathed.

"I can…. You can…," the fox stammered.

"It's alright," the rabbit muttered as she turned her head, exposing her neck more. The two creatures' hearts hammered in their chests. The fox continued to behave gentlemanly as he continued his work and finished without incident. As the fox turned toward the gunny sack, the pair let out breaths they didn't realize they were holding. Neither heard anything over the sound of their own hearts beating and rapid breathing.

The fox pulled out a fox mask and a rope fashioned with fox fluff shaped into a false tail.

"Put this mask on and wrap this around your waist," the fox instructed. The rabbit held the mask in her paws. It was made from cypress wood and was light but sturdy. She could also tell that, despite being recently cleaned, the mask itself was old.

"You can't be serious!" the rabbit exclaimed.

"It was the only one I had, and you won't be the only one wearing one," the fox assured her. The rabbit relented and placed the mask over her face. She then wrapped the fox fluff rope around her waist like a belt. The fox then adjusted it so that it covered her tail. It appeared she had a fox's tail.

"I'm guessing I won't be the only one who will be wearing their tail like this?" she asked.

"It's a little vintage, but nobody will question it," the fox replied. He retrieved a small looking glass from the gunny sack and handed it to her.

"What do you think?" the fox asked.

The rabbit looked at herself. "I can't believe I look so different. I don't look like myself, but I'm not quite a fox either. Are you sure this will work?"

"It won't not work." The fox averted his eyes. He turned and started away.

"Come on. Sun's setting, and the festival is starting," the fox called to her.

The rabbit stood there for a moment. Then taking a calming breath, she started after him. The fox slowed his pace until they were walking side by side. The fox attempted to reach for her paw before deciding against it. He snapped his paw back. His action did not go unnoticed by the rabbit.

Chapter 7

The Festival Begins

*E*ven with her ears tied down, the rabbit heard the festival before she saw it. The music was playing loudly, and there were shouts, laughter, and a multitude of voices talking to each other. Once the pair reached the clearing, the rabbit dropped her jaw in astonishment. Never had she seen so many animals in one place, let alone foxes. The vulpine came in all shapes, sizes, and colors. They were scattered, moving, and dancing inside the clearing. Torches lined the glade, and a variety of lanterns hung from the surrounding trees.

A small group of foxes in black robes lit a string of lights along the perimeter of the clearing. The way the lights swayed made them look like a jubilee of dancing fireflies. As the sun was setting, the twinkling stars aided with the flickering candles in lighting the festival. There were seven fire pits—six lined the corners of the clearing and the biggest one in the center. The only one that was lit sat closest to the banquet table.

The banquet table itself was longer than the height of the surrounding trees and stuffed with every food imaginable. The aroma of fresh baked bread spread through the clearing. The intoxicating scent ranged from French to Sourdough to Pita. A variety of finger foods sat on huge serving trays. Mouth-watering crackers covered in spreads made of cheese, fruit, and a few things the rabbit couldn't identify, such as tiny black spheres, objects wrapped in meat and skewered, mini quiches, assorted sliders, baked balls filled with meat, and cheese and vegetables. The middle of the table held various roasts and meat: ham, roast beef, chicken, goat, a rack of lamb, and even an entire turkey.

Surrounding the meat were sauces, gravy, and a jar of mint jelly. Fresh and baked fruits, like grapes, bananas, oranges, kiwis, plantains, dragon fruit, mangos, huckleberries, blueberries, and strawberries followed the meats. Between the fresh fruits and the desserts were pickled peaches, pickled apples, pickled okra, pickled carrots, pickled onions, pickled eggs, pickled beets, and even pickled cucumbers.

The dessert table was in a league of its own. Full sized cakes, pies, and cookies filled every available space. Flowers made of frosting decorated the vases, waiting to be picked. Sweetened bread and cobblers lined the outer rim of the table. At the end, there were even marshmallows, chocolates, and graham crackers for any fox--large or small--to make smores.

While it didn't seem possible, foxes dressed in colored aprons added more food to the overflowing table. More foxes arrived, bringing their own homemade dishes and placing them in any available space. On the other side of the fire, a large band sat softly playing their instruments. A deep red vixen stood as if mesmerized with her bow that seemed to float over her violin. A portly tod thumped his drum in a steady beat. A tall fox played a flute as skinny as he was. Several other musicians, including a handsome tod carrying a large wooden instrument and an attractive vixen, stood at the outskirts, talking to friends before the festival revved up full swing. A lone tod wearing a pinned rose sat off by himself, staring at the torch in front of him as if in a trance. He reached down and kissed his rose before repining it to his chest and gripping his horn for dear life.

Despite waiting for the party to go into full swing, the music could be heard in every corner of the glade. A few couples, both teenagers and older pairs, took the opportunity to slow dance in the clear area. Young kits also danced off-rhythm in front of the band. A platform set up in front of the fire pit in the center of the clearing stood vacant.

All the various vulpine were in their own little groups, talking to old friends or trying to make new ones. The rabbit struggled to keep her breathing in check. A paw came into her field of vision. The fox had offered her his paw, shooting her a reassuring glance. Taking one final deep breath, she grasped the fox's paw, and they stepped over the black soil barrier separating the clearing from the trees.

The rabbit could hear her heart pound in her ears as they weaved through the various vulpine groups. Old friends and long-lost family members embraced left and right. Wannabe Casanovas and poser sirens approached groups of the opposing gender, trying to attract a dance partner. Most were unsuccessful as their recipients were either apathetic or oblivious. Families tried to wrangle their little kits, who wanted to run in all directions.

A rogue kit ran past her, almost knocking her down. The kit half muttered an apology before heading towards the dessert table. It was at that moment that the rabbit became very aware of her own feet. They were larger than all the foxes surrounding her, and she knew a wild paw stepping on her would surely blow her cover.

She was about to sprint away when the music died, and a loud voice boomed through the clearing.

"Greetings and welcome, my fine fellow foxes!" A fox who had begun to gray around his whiskers was now standing on the stage, addressing the festival attendees. "It's great to have you all here, whether it is your first time, third, twentieth, or your first in a long time. We gather here to rekindle the spirit that lights up our lives and the lives of those around us."

The rabbit looked around. All foxes big and small were listening intently to the Elder vulpine.

"Now the head chef has informed me that the banquet table is finally ready. So, let's all bow our heads in blessing, and I can get out of y'all's way." All foxes bowed their heads as the speaker said grace. The rabbit followed suit. When he finished, the spokesperson declared, "Let the festival begin!"

All the foxes split towards the banquet table or the dance floor. The music had picked back up and was well underway with couples and individuals dancing in earnest. The rabbit followed her fox as he led her to the banquet table. The line split with her being on the side opposite the tree line. She made her way down the long table, selecting fruits and vegetables, as well as a few cakes she recognized.

"Don't!" someone exclaimed as the rabbit reached toward what appeared to be a cake with jelly on it. She quickly withdrew her hand.

"Sorry." The tod apologized, but not before grabbing the last of the jelly cake. "I know they're going to bring out more, but I've been waiting all year for these."

"It's fine," the rabbit choked out.

The fox muttered a thanks, but she ignored him. She continued down the table despite no longer picking up more food.

"Here," the tod said, offering her a plate she couldn't have reached from her side of the table. Eyeing the plate, a lump rose in her throat.

The plate was loaded with roasted quail.

"No thanks," she choked out.

"You sure?" the tod asked. The rabbit nodded her head.

"Suit yourself." He shrugged his shoulders and loaded his plate. "Grapes and quail!"

"Grapes and quail," the rabbit weakly repeated. The tod gave her an approving nod before slipping away.

Once she reached the end of the table, she saw her fox and quickly made her way toward him. She would tell him that she must slip away at the earliest possibility without drawing attention to herself. She had just reached him when....

"River, my boy!" An older fox with strong arms and sparkling eyes approached. He escorted his elderly vixen.

The older tod reached his paw toward the rabbit's fox. As the younger tod extended his paw, the elderly fox turned his hand sideways and made a gesture with the outstretched appendage.

"Turkey!" he proclaimed proudly.

"Never gets old." The younger tod rolled his eyes.

"Just like my wife!"

"Oh, stop it, you." The vixen to his left playfully smacked his distended belly.

"It's true." The older fox laughed. He glanced over at the masked rabbit. "And who is this little thing?"

"I'm sorry," the fox said to everyone, "This is Cedar." He indicated the masked rabbit next him, "Cedar, this is Clark and Lana." "A pleasure to meet you, dear," Lana greeted, replacing the cane in her right paw with the rabbit's. She leaned on her husband as she steadied herself.

"Yes, dear, a pleasure," Clark said. The masked rabbit moved to present her paw to the older tod, who responded by placing his paw under hers with his two index claws sticking out. "SNAIL!"

"You're lucky I don't whack you with this," Lana brandished her cane.

"Come on," Clark pleaded. "These are youngins and need to learn the classics."

"And it is a party," The younger tod snapped back.

"The kit is right," Clark declared. "Grapes and quail!"

"Grapes and quail!" The other foxes in the group and a lone fox walking by the group chorused.

"Grapes and quail," the masked rabbit stated weakly, a beat behind the vulpine. This did not go unnoticed by the elderly couple.

"She hasn't heard the story of grapes and quail?" Clark asked the younger tod.

"Her parents were practicalists," the rabbit's fox answered quickly.

"If it wasn't in front of them, it might as well not exist."

"Stringents, I hear you. Been there, done that, and don't recommend it." Clark nodded and shook his head in agreement. He turned his head toward the masked rabbit. "Have you ever heard of 'sour grapes'?"

The rabbit thought for a moment and guessed, "Taste the grapes before you pick all of them to make sure they're not sour?"

"Good advice, but not what we're talking about," Clark stated.

"The story of sour grapes begins with a fox walking through the woods when he comes across a quail eating grapes atop a wall." Clark turned to Lana. "I forget, was the wall made of ivory or covered in ivy?"

"I think both."

"Anyway," Clark began again, "the fox asked the quail what he was eating. The quail responded, 'I'll show you, only because it will torment you.' The quail dropped a grape to the fox and the fox found it delicious. The fox asked for more and the quail said no, so the fox offered payment, and the quail refused again. The fox threatened him, and the quail laughed. The fox began jumping up the wall to get the grapes and the quail. The quail continued to laugh and eat the grapes from the vine. Finally, the fox exhausted himself. The quail mocked him, saying the grapes he ate were a little sour, and then he flew away."

"You know I have heard of sour grapes, but I didn't know the story or what it meant. Wait, why is it a saying of celebration when the fox faces misfortune?" The rabbit wore a confused expression.

"Because only foxes know the second part of the story." Clark plucked a roasted quail from his own plate and dipped it in the sauce to the side. "The fox waited until the grapes grew back and climbed a tree that overlooked the ivory wall. Sure enough, that quail returned to eat the grapes, and the fox pounced on him and ate him in one bite!" Clark punctuated this by eating his own quail in one bite. "The fox spent the rest of the day eating the grapes, lounging on top of the ivory wall, and thinking to himself that nothing had ever been sweeter." Clark gave a flourish and licked the flavor from his claws. Lana smiled and shook her head at her husband's antics.

"Why don't other animals know the full story?" the rabbit asked before biting her tongue. She had just given away more information than she intended. Luckily, the foxes didn't notice.

"You know how it is. Birds get around far more, and once they open their trap, they never close it," Clark said nonchalantly. "And no matter what we do, people don't trust foxes."

"Which is a shame," Lana said, "With all the food the festival provides, others could enjoy it too. Badgers, beavers, and heck, even an entire family of rabbits could eat, and there would still be leftovers."

"First, beavers would be more interested in biting the table than the food on it. Second, the rabbits would be scared off by the big vat of rabbit stew!" Clark chuckled.

"We haven't had rabbit stew in years. The guys got sick of bringing the stone cauldron up, keeping it lit all seven nights, and then taking it down again," the rabbit's fox said.

"Considering it took at least four tods to carry it, I don't blame them," Clark observed. "You think the pain would be in the legs, but it's your lower back that takes the brunt of it. I couldn't wag my tail right for weeks, and of course, there's always someone stepping on it."

"Speaking of which, I love what you've done with yours," Lana said, addressing the masked rabbit.

The rabbit was still trying to process the rabbit stew comment that she hadn't paid attention to Lana's observation.

"What?" she asked.

"Your tail," Lana indicated the rabbit's faux fur tail. "It looks nice."

"I'm sorry. Thank you," the rabbit stammered.

"They haven't worn their tails like that since I was a young vixen," Lana said wistfully.

"Who said you weren't still?" Clark asked her with a playful grin.

"Oh, stop it, you." Blushing, Lana gave him another playful

"Attention, everyone!" A voice rang through the clearing. The band died, and all foxes dropped to silence in mid-conversation. The torches and lanterns had kept everything so bright, the rabbit hadn't noticed the sun had gone down.

"It is time for our legends to live on!" announced the Elder fox whose gray fur shone like silver.

All the foxes, including the masked rabbit and her fox, made their way to stand in front of the stage. The older fox with gray around his whiskers came out into the center.

"It is time to remember the stories that keep us going. The ones that inspire, teach, and remind us of the important things we hold dear in this life and the next," the Elder fox declared.

"We will start as we always have with the first ever fox fire......"

Chapter 8
The Herald of Winter

Once there was a valley, quiet like this one, where winter never seemed to come to the clearing. The sun always shone, the grass continued to grow, and the trees bore fruit year-round. Life was peaceful for the inhabitants. Until one day, a young tod felt a stir in the air.

He felt the wind change and bring a chill that blew past his ears and down his back. The fox knew that winter was coming. He stood on the largest stump he could find and yelled, "Everyone, winter is coming! We must prepare!"

The other animals replied, "Winter never comes to the valley! It hasn't been cold in years."

Some grew suspicious of him. "The fox is trying to trick us. He will steal our food after we stockpile it!"

Others openly mocked him. "Everyone, look at the fox, the new herald of winter."

The fox persisted, but soon the other animals dispersed. The fox was sullen. His attempt to help had only brought ridicule.

"I felt it too," he heard a voice say. The fox turned to see an old badger, black as night.

"You felt the cold?" the fox asked.

And I've felt it before. In a week's time, the entire valley will be covered in snow and ice." The badger gestured to the space around him. "Why didn't you agree with me? Why didn't you tell everyone what was coming?" the fox asked.

"They wouldn't have believed me, the same way they didn't believe you. You just watch. The others will go about their daily lives, and by the time the snow falls, it will be too late."

"Well, I can't fix everyone else," the fox replied simply, "but I can fix me."

Every day the next week, the fox prepared for the approaching winter by stocking food, clean water, firewood, and all other essentials. He reinforced his hollow to withstand the cold. He cleaned his chimney and airways to ensure proper airflow. As he made his preparations, he observed the other animals of the valley. True to what the badger said, they lived their lives as normal. Bunnies played tag in the meadow while sniffing the wildflowers. A porcupine lazed in the sun next to the stream. A mother robin took twigs out of her nest to get a better cross breeze.

Most ignored him and his actions. Others believed he was still trying to trick them. "He is hoping we will follow his example and then steal from us once we have gathered our food."

Others continued to mock him. "Your food will spoil, and your wood will rot before you have a chance to use it."

He didn't argue, he listened calmly, and then he stood on top of the stump once more and proclaimed, "Everyone, winter is coming! We must prepare before it is too late!"

Again, the other animals ignored and mocked him.

Once they left, the fox sat in front of the stump and slumped against it.

"What did I tell you?" he heard a voice again. The same old black badger came over carrying food and firewood.

"This valley will die," the fox said solemnly.

"No, it won't," the badger replied. "The animals might, but spring will come again, and this valley will be reborn. I've seen it once, I'll see it again, and God willing, I'll see it a third time."

"The other animals won't be as lucky," the fox replied.

"Well, what can you do?" the old black badger asked.

That was a good question. What could the fox do?

The next morning, a heavy frost settled over the valley. When the sun rose, a multitude of rays glittered over every surface. The animals of the valley woke and began to panic.

"Winter hasn't come in years, and now it will come all at once!!!!"

All the animals scrambled to make their preparations. They picked berry bushes clean, climbed over each other to get water from the stream, and gathered any loose sticks or branches they could find. The fox frowned at the scenes that played out in front of him.

"This is madness," he said.

"This is survival," the old black badger waddled up beside him.

Above them, they could hear the mother robin weeping and chirping for all to hear. "What will I do? I have already laid my eggs! I will freeze come winter, and so will my children."

"We've got to do something," the fox told the old black badger.

"What is there to do?" the old black badger asked. "Once the sun sets tonight, it won't rise again until the springtime. Today is all anyone has."

"So, the sun's working against us?" the fox inquired.

"Since you already seem to know everything, let me give you some advice," the old black badger said. "No matter how strong or smart or fortunate you are, you can't attain more sunlight."

The fox looked towards the westernmost mountain, where the sun disappears when it sets.

"Then I'll just have to create some."

As the last of the sunlight peaked over the westernmost mountain, most animals scrambled to get one last twig, one last berry, one last cup of water before winter descended on the valley. Others looked over their current haul and silently knew it wouldn't be enough. Mothers tried to soothe their frightened children. Loners tried to reassure themselves.

Some broke down in tears.

The sun finally disappeared over the mountains, and the animals prepared to be cloaked in darkness. But they opened their eyes to find the land still clear around them. They looked to the westernmost mountain, and near its peak roared a fire that cast a light over the entire valley. Nobody had time to question what was happening as they hastily continued their preparations.

"Why are you doing this?" the badger asked the fox as the tod threw more logs on the fire.

"God give me strength," the fox prayed as he carried larger and larger logs to the fire he had created.

"Why are you doing this?" the badger asked once more.

"I can't let this valley die, not if I can help it," the fox answered, straining against the weight of his newest log.

He then fell to the ground under the weight of a large beam. Heaving it aside, he stood up and cried out to heaven. "God! If you can, hear me! If you're even there! I beg you! Please let your grace and mercy shine down on this valley! Please!" he cried out. He fell to his knees. "I can't do this; not without you!" he sobbed.

Taking a deep breath, the fox stood up and grabbed the beam with renewed strength and carried it to the fire.

"Ahhh…. You are crazy …." the old black badger mumbled to himself before grabbing a log himself and joining the fox.

The animals down below continued to complete their preparations. They would emerge the following spring far thinner, but they would emerge. They began helping each other as they scrambled to make sure everyone finished the tasks and was prepared. Others went up the mountain to help maintain the fire. Even with some help, the fox continued to carry logs that weighed more than he did. Sweat and flames stung his eyes. His body fought against fatigue, the heat of the fire, and the nighttime chill.

Finally, all the preparations were made, and the animals climbed up the mountain. The last one was a lone squirrel who declared, "The mother robin's nest has been reinforced, and she has enough acorns to last until spring!"

"Is that everyone?" someone asked. The animals all looked around and found that everyone was accounted for and ready for winter.

"Who is the one who started this fire? Who is the one who has saved us?" they asked.

All eyes turned to the very exhausted fox, who only now had allowed himself to rest.

"Let us thank and celebrate him!" the animals cried out. They opened their arms to welcome him.

Instead, the fox broke his way through the crowd and started heading back to his hollow. Before he left, he gave these parting words, "I'll see you all in the spring."

Chapter 9

Ashes

A hush came over the audience as the Elder fox completed the story. Within a second, the silence was broken by thunderous applause.

Even the rabbit clapped along with everyone else.

When the applause died down, the gray whiskered fox announced.

"Thank you for listening! Enjoy the rest of tonight, and I'll see you all tomorrow." One last round of applause accompanied the gray whiskered fox as he made his way off the stage.

The group around the stage began to disperse. The band took this as a cue to burst forth into music. The fox with the horn broke his focus from the torch, brought the horn to his brims and began to play like a creature possessed. Gone was the steady flow, now replaced by a gushing tide of enchanting melodies.

Couples drifted to the dance floor as the music picked back up. Foxes with a sweet tooth returned to the table to pile a plate high with desserts. A few broke into smaller groups to talk with friends, old and new. Little kits grabbed marshmallows and sticks to roast them by the firepit. A few elders stood by the fire to warm their old bones and ensure the younglings safety from being burned.

The masked rabbit and her fox meandered to the threshold between the woods and the dance floor. They stood silent as foxes filtered in and out as the volume and tempo of the music rose and fell. Out of the corner of her eye, she could see her fox swaying to the music. A small part of her thought of asking him to dance; however, every instinct, gut feeling, and rational thought told her to run. For whatever reason, she stayed rooted to her spot near her fox.

A flirty vixen made her way to the odd couple. "Care to dance, Mr. Riverbank?"

"I'm good, Jazz," the rabbit's fox replied.

"What about you?" the vixen named Jazz turned to the masked rabbit. "You've got a handsome tod all to yourself, and you aren't going to dance with him?"

Before the masked rabbit could answer, the fox stepped in, "She's not much of a dancer, and I don't feel like dancing."

"Your loss," Jazz shot a flirty, mischievous look over her shoulder as she turned away. The masked rabbit didn't know if it was directed at her or the tod.

"I have to go," the rabbit turned away suddenly.

"I'll come with you," the fox said, grabbing a dim side lantern.

The rabbit wanted to refuse but instead started walking with the fox beside her. After a while, the rabbit broke the silence.

"I'll admit that it wasn't what I was expecting," the rabbit said.

"How so?" the fox asked.

"I just figured that since it was telling the story of the first fire festival, it would end as a festival with the fox being thanked and celebrated," the rabbit admitted.

"Foxes aren't used to being thanked." He grinned to himself, "And glory's overrated."

"I guess," the rabbit relented, a puzzled expression hid under her mask. They continued walking until they reached the clearing with trees without bark.

"So...," the fox stammered uneasily, "I guess I'll ... see you tomorrow?"

"Sure," the rabbit stated plainly.

She parted ways, wondering if they would see each other again.

Chapter 10

Fate and Destiny

The fox nervously stoked the fire. He knew his plan was a long shot, if not downright crazy, but he had been optimistic. At the very least, there would have been a more definitive ending than her just not showing up. He got up to gather cedar wood for the fourth time. He had collected enough for the rest of the week the second time and picked the surrounding area clean after the third time. Still, the work gave him an excuse to keep checking the perimeter and kept him from going completely stir crazy. After checking his pile twice and adding a few measly twigs, he returned to his fire.

The light from the sky was fading, so the fire either needed more wood or to be doused. He reached into his sack for his water jug when he heard rustling. He turned to see the rabbit shambling into the clearing, mask askew, faux tail loose, and looking disheveled.

"What happened?" the concerned fox asked.

The masked rabbit huffed, "What you're seeing is the result of me trying to apply the disguise by myself." She spread her arms to fully display the fruits of her labor.

The fox let out a sigh of relief that morphed into an amused chuckle. "You look like you got dressed in the dark."

The rabbit looked dejected. "How bad is it?"

"Well, your fur's a mess, your mask is half off your face, and your tail is hanging off the wrong side," the fox observed.

The rabbit chuckled to herself. "I'm guessing you never met a fox with their tail like that?"

"If I did, I'd be concerned." The fox snickered. He then proceeded to douse the flames and start the routine of applying the cedar cinder and fixing the rest of her disguise. The rabbit complied and moved as was needed. She showed little hesitation as the fox applied the cinders to her neck.

"How can someone be this bad at dressing themselves?" the fox mused.

The rabbit huffed, "I did my best. I tried to use the brook as a makeshift mirror, and it wouldn't stay still."

"And it won't be quiet either." The fox looked up at the rabbit. "It's always babbling."

It was the worst joke the rabbit had ever heard, but she laughed anyway. It started as a light chuckle, and before long, both had erupted into side-splitting laughter.

Once they calmed down, the fox helped the rabbit readjust her mask. He then held out his paw, which she took, and led her back to the festival grounds.

As the odd couple crossed the threshold into the festival clearing, the rabbit noticed some differences. A second bonfire roared high and mighty, and the foxes had taken measures to spruce themselves up by adorning themselves with bright colors. Many a vixen wore flowers in their fur. Scarves of several colors adorned the necks of dozens. Quite a few wore fox masks, some plain, others with elaborate designs and patterns. A large crate sat in front of the second bonfire, overflowing with wooden masks. To its side was a station designated to paint them.

Paw traffic flowed constantly between the crate and station.

"Looks like I'm going to fit in tonight," the masked rabbit observed.

"If your tail doesn't give you away," the fox retorted. The rabbit shot a glance down at her waist before realizing her faux tail was perfect. She shot her fox an annoyed glare. The fox responded with a smirk, "We should get some food, even though we were late and missed the blessing."

"Kit, is that you?" A caramel-colored fox wearing what looked like a gray collared jacket approached the odd pair.

"Baset!" the fox beamed. The two tods embraced.

"How have you been, Kit?" Baset asked. He spoke with the remnants of an accent that the rabbit couldn't quite place.

The fox shook his head, "I'm never going to outgrow that, am I?"

"Not even when you're old and gray," Baset mused. He turned to the masked rabbit. "And who's this little vixen?"
"This is Cedar," the fox introduced his companion.

The masked rabbit held out her paw, "Pleased to meet you, Mr. Bouset?"

The rabbit's fox snorted. Baset shot him a glance. "It's actually Baset, Bass-Set."

"I'm sorry," the masked rabbit said.

"Don't be! Most call me Bast, like fast, the first time they hear it," Baset shot the fox another glance, "and some Kits, who shall remain nameless, will continue to do so even when it stops being funny."

"There you are!" a vixen called. The new vixen had fur the color of honey and was escorting two younger identical foxlings.

Baset grinned. "Ridley, you remember my wife, Xin."

As the honey-colored fox joined the group, it became clear that the family came as a matching set. Standing together, it was apparent that the caramel-colored fox and the honey-colored vixen had littered a set of identical kits with hazel-colored eyes. The kits were on the cusp of adolescence and came up to their parents' chests. Despite being male and female, the kits had matching faces with the only discernable difference being their ears. The male had a black tipped left ear, and the female's was tipped on her right ear.

Their clothes matched their parents more closely than each other. Baset wore a gray jacket with a black collar. His son wore a matching black jacket with a gray collar. Xin wore a loose-fitting red dress with a gold sash. Her daughter wore a matching gold dress with a red sash.

"Great to see you," the rabbit's fox clasped his paws together. "None of that," Xin said as she pulled the fox into a big hug. She inhaled deeply. "It's good to know the young kit still gives the best hugs." Xin spoke with the same remnants of an accent as her husband, but her voice reverberated as if her throat were coated in honey.

"I try," the fox responded. Xin turned her attention to the masked rabbit. "And who might this be?"

"This is Cedar," the rabbit's fox replied. "Cedar, this is the lovely Xin, and her kits are the beautiful Delia and the handsome Felix." The kits bowed at being introduced.

"It's a pleasure to meet all of you," the masked rabbit started to bow in response. Before she could react, she was swept into the embrace of the honey-colored fox. The vixen deeply inhaled the masked rabbit's scent as she hugged her. The masked rabbit's shock turned to terror as a thousand biological alerts activated at once. Her heart hammered in her chest as every instinct told her to run and run fast and not look back.

"Cedar..." Xin said as she broke the embrace. The masked rabbit's head screamed for her to flee, but her feet had turned to lead.

"You smell.... just like cedar wood," Xin observed.

"No surprise, since Cedar grew up in the hollow roots of a cedar tree." The rabbit's fox quickly came to her aid.

"That explains it," Xin beamed. "I hope she didn't burn any."

"My mother thought that cedar wood sap was the cure for everything," the masked rabbit blurted. "She would've had me bathe in it, if it were possible."

"I heard the sap can clean wounds when mixed with a little honey," Xin stated.

"I've never heard of that, but I'm willing to try it," Baset said.

"Attention, everyone!" a voice rang out through the clearing.

"That's our cue," Baset said. Before they knew it, the odd pair were whisked away with the colorful family of foxes. They soon found themselves meshed with the vibrant kin in a sea of vulpine.

"It is time to remember the stories that keep us going. The stories that inspire, teach, and remind us of the important things we hold dear in this life and the next," the Elder fox declared.

"This tale comes from the east, where the light of the moon bridges a way between the stars ...."

Chapter 11

Dancing on the Starlight Bridge

There once was a young tod who liked to sit by the forest pond and watch the night sky. Late at night, he would find his special spot in the roots of the great oak tree and watch the night sky light up with stars.

He would trace the constellations in the dirt, record the movement of planets, and count the shooting stars. His favorite thing, however, was when the moonlight broke through the clouds and hit the forest pond creating a shimmering path on the water.

He imagined that it acted as a stairway to the heavens he adored so much. One night during the full moon, an angelic figure appeared on the moonlit water. After a regal bow, the vision began to dance on the water's surface. The angelic being was stiff and practiced at first, with curtsies and practiced poses, but then flowed freely and naturally with jumps and spins.

The tod was entranced. Never had anyone seen such beauty and grace. He watched for what seemed like forever. Then the moon started to dip under the trees. The figure's dancing space got smaller and smaller until she performed one final curtsy. She then looked directly at the young fox and smiled. The tod was floored, and he was about to call out to her, when the being disappeared in a cascade of shimmering light.

He returned to the spot for many years and waited for the being to return. Every full moon when the light hit the water, the celestial maiden would return and perform her dance. The tod was entranced each time and committed her moves to memory. During the day, he would mirror them as best he could. He would often imagine them dancing together as partners if he had the guts to ask her to dance.

One night when the tod had reached maturity, he plucked up the courage to address the maiden directly. When the moonlight hit the water, the celestial maiden appeared once more. Emerging from his special spot, the handsome tod rose to address her. Before he could speak, the maiden called to him.

"Hello," she greeted.

The tod blinked back in surprise. "Hello," he called back.

"Come to see me dance?" she inquired.

"Actually, for the longest time I've wanted to join you," he answered.

The maiden walked on the moonlight towards him. As she stood in front of him, his breath was taken away. Starlight radiated from her being in the warmest of glows. She was even more enchanting up close.

She smiled at him. "Can you dance?"

"I hope so."

The maiden reached out to him. "Join me," The tod took her paw in his and stepped onto the surface of the pond. He was amazed when he did not sink. Standing on the surface of moonlight, the fox was nervous, excited, dumbfounded, and spellbound as he held the maiden he had admired for so long in his arms.

"Let us begin," the maiden said taking her first sidestep. The fox broke from his stupor and matched her movement. She continued her routine with the fox being her perfect complement. She was the picture, and he was the frame. The pair exemplified grace as they carefully stepped only on the moonlight. They continued to dance even when the routine ended. The maiden let the fox spin her, dip her, and lift her over his head. To him, she was lighter than air.

The moon continued to dip under the trees as they danced. Their dance space grew smaller, and the maiden took the opportunity to move closer to her dance partner. The space shrank until the pair could only hold each other and sway.

The maiden looked into the eyes of the fox. "I've been watching you, you know. As you watch the heavens, my starlight has been shining down, lighting the wonder in your eyes." She caressed his face. "I'm glad I got to see it up close."

"I swear," the fox began, "that as long as I live, I'll meet you here under the full moon, and we will dance as we did tonight."

The celestial maiden's face fell. "Tonight was my last night. After tonight, I will be unable to return." She looked at the fox with eyes brimming with tears that had yet to fall. "You could come with me and become a star yourself. I know you have a life…"

The maiden was cut off as the fox pulled her into his embrace and buried his face into her neck. "Where you go, I go," he mumbled. The maiden closed her eyes as twin tears of joy streamed down her cheeks.

As the moonlight faded from the pond, the maiden and her fox shimmered before ascending to the heavens, becoming two stars together forever in the night sky.

Chapter 12

Picking Star Gazers

A reverent silence fell over the crowd. Vixens, young and old, were starstruck and their eyes gleamed. Others pulled their partners close and wrapped their tails around each other. Some had been in that position since before the story began. Then a round of applause swept over the crowd.

"That story always makes my heart flutter," Xin said.

"My heart should be fluttering because I have a celestial maiden right here," Baset pulled his wife close. Xin giggled at her husband's affections as Baset nuzzled her neck.

"Mom! Dad!" The embarrassed twins objected in unison.

Once the couple broke apart, they wrangled their kits and the odd couple towards the dance floor. Couples had already started pairing up. Masked gents enticed young vixens to let them be whisked away. Disguised beauties lured their chosen tods into their embrace. Within minutes, the air was filled with music, and colors flew in all directions. Bright yellows, vibrant greens, stunning reds, royal purples, ember oranges, and deep blues all spun and twirled along with their host who moved in practiced rhythms.

"You two should ask a nice kit to dance with you," Xin addressed the foxlings. Delia politely declined. Felix scrunched his face in disgust.

"Young one, you have jelly on your face." Xin pulled out a kerchief to wipe her son's face. Felix struggled at his mother's attention.

"So will you two be dancing?" Baset addressed the masked rabbit and her fox.

"Ummm…." the odd couple stammered.

"You better snatch him up quickly, Cedar. I've heard some vixens asking about him," Baset teased.

"Cedar, dear, you have ash on your neck." Xin turned from her now clean-faced son and advanced on the cinder-stained rabbit. "Here's a napkin so you can wipe it off." The rabbit froze in place, her heart hammering, and her legs telling her to run.

"She can't," the rabbit's fox threw himself between the two.

"Why not?" Xin queried with a puzzled expression.

"Umm..umm..ummmm." The masked rabbit's mouth refused to form words.

"There was a fire," the rabbit's fox spat out.

"Yes," the masked rabbit finally choked out.

"The ash covers her burn marks, and she's very sensitive about them," the rabbit's fox added.

"Oh," Xin's puzzlement melted into concern. "I'm so sorry dear."

"It's — it's nothing," the masked rabbit mumbled before storming off past the edge of the clearing.

"She's nice, but you can't force things," Baset said. "There's always that initial attraction, but for it to keep going there has to be that one moment where everything lines up. Love will fill up, you won't be able to stop smiling, and your life's never the same. Problem is love like that takes nothing short of destiny."

"I think there's more to it than that," the fox said. He then followed the masked rabbit.

The fox found the masked rabbit sitting on a log on the outer rim of the festival, where few ever walked. The fox sat on the right side of the rabbit. After a moment of silence, he spoke up.

"It was close," the fox said. "She almost smelled you."

"Apparently, I also have burn marks," the rabbit mused humorlessly.

"Baset won't tell, and not many will judge you based on injuries," the fox reassured.

"That's not the point!" the rabbit exclaimed harshly. "My disguise, my history, and even my name you pulled out of thin air. I'm nobody, and yet everything about me puts me in danger! My heart feels like it's going to beat straight out of my chest!"

"Out of your back," the fox stated.

The rabbit looked at him, perplexed. "What?" she asked.

"Your heart can't beat out of your chest because your ribcage and breastplate prevent it. If it was going to beat out, it would exit your back."

The rabbit gave the fox the most blank yet judgmental look someone was ever able to convey through a mask. "Know a lot about rabbit anatomy, do you?"

"It's not just rabbits. It's all creatures with fur, same four legs, same red blood, same ribcage with a heart in it." The fox gave the rabbit an awkward but earnest smile. The rabbit turned away as the ground had somehow become far more interesting. The odd pair sat in silence once more.

"I have an idea," the fox stated.

"Is it as good as your others?" the rabbit asked sardonically.

"Maybe," the fox said. "How about we talk, and you tell me about yourself?"

The rabbit looked at him puzzled, "Why do you want to do that?"

"I figured it's better to cover for you if we're not just, as you so eloquently put it, pulling your identity out of thin air," the fox scorned.

The rabbit looked down and patiently asked, "How do we start?"

The fox thought for a moment, "Alright, honest answer. Do you think that love is like Baset and Xin said, as spontaneous and powerful as being struck by lightning?"

The rabbit remained silent. The fox spoke up. "You don't have to worry because we're the only ones here and I won't judge…."

"It's not that," Ceder interrupted. "I was just thinking." She remained silent for another moment.

"Between the two, I still think I'm more likely to be struck by lightning than fall in love," she stated.

"So, no love at first sight?" the fox asked.

"Love's not that simple. It doesn't just happen. It must grow over time, be worked on, and cared for. Like...," the rabbit was lost for words.

"A tree?" the fox supplied.

"Exactly," the rabbit confirmed. "The tree as strong and sturdy as an oak or a redwood doesn't just spring up overnight. It takes years to become what it is." She turned back to the fox. "What about you? Is love quick or gradual?"

"I wouldn't really know from personal experience. I haven't really felt either in my life." He paused. "At least nothing as profound as what we are talking about." He paused once more. "And I'm not sure where to go from here."

The odd pair sat in silence for several moments. The only noises came from the soft tunes coming from the other side of the festival and the light chirping of insects.

"My name is Estella," she said.

"Stella?"

"E-stella with an E." She rolled her eyes. This clearly wasn't the first time she had made the distinction.

"Okay, why E-stella?" She sighed.

"I was the sixth-born child of my parents' fifth litter. Rabbits traditionally name all kittens of the same litter with the same first letter and usually go in alphabetical order."

"I guess that helps keep track of things, having so many kittens and all," the fox replied.

"It's also considered bad luck to do it in a random order and practically dooming yourself to do it in reverse," Estella said.

"Are bunnies typically superstitious?"

"Fearful is the better word, since we typically run from anything that could be the least bit dangerous," she admitted.

"You didn't."

Estella shrugged her shoulders. "I don't know what to tell you."

The fox thought for a moment, "So, you're the sixth born of the fifth litter. Where does that put you in the pecking order?"

Estella chuckled humorlessly. "In the absolute worst possible position. Technically, I'm one of the older siblings since I'm in the fifth out of eleven litters, so I'm expected to help take care of my younger siblings, but not so old as to get any respect or recognition. I've got one of the heaviest loads on one of the steeper inclines."

"I'm guessing that's how you got to be so independent," the fox stated.

Estella snorted. "Independence? No such thing. We are all one big kerfuffle. Our entire lives are built around adding to and maintaining the pile. You only get to leave to start your own. The primary and only rule is that family comes first." She gave one last joyless huff and then remained silent as the fox let her breathe.

"Speaking of loads," the fox finally asked, "How many kittens do bunnies usually have?"

"Total, or at a time?" Estella queried.

"Either," the fox said with a shocked expression.

"The typical litter is five to eight at a time, but mine was ten. The number of litters is as many as a couple can carry out, but I've never heard of anybody making it past N. As for the total, the number fluctuates until keeping a total is pointless. However, I can safely say my family total is one." Estella's head drooped.

"I'm sorry," the fox said after a while.

"It's nothing," Estella replied. She turned to the fox, "What about you? I've heard people call you Kit, Ridley, River, and Riverbank. What's your real name?"

The fox smiled at the brim. "Kit means youngling, but I haven't felt young in a long time. The name my mother gave me was Ridley. She always told me it was because love is a riddle, and she couldn't figure out how she loved me so much from the first time she saw me." Ridley leaned back in reminiscence, "Riverbank is from my youth. Whenever I played with other foxlings, I'd always say let's go to the river to swim. It became a bit of a default for me, so everyone started calling me Riverbank Ridley or just River for short."

Estella gave him a small smile through her mask. "Why did you like the river so much?"

Ridley chuckled, "This will sound strange, but I love the feeling of water on my skin. I love the way the water feels when waves wash over my paw pads. I love watching minnows swim in the shallow water. I love being underwater, in that other world hiding just below the surface. When I swam, I used to not come up for air until I absolutely needed to. It used to scare my mom half to death."

Estella grinned at him. "Sounds like you were a momma's kit."

"No more than any other tod, and what can I say?" Ridley replied. "I love my momma."

Estella gave a contented sigh as she stared at the fox. She noticed that this was the first time she had seen him truly at ease. It looked good on him.

After a while, she asked, "Speaking of your mom, how many siblings do you have?"

"I'm the oldest, so two younger siblings, first, a boy and then a girl."

"Is that a lot?" Estella inquired.

"Two is conservative, five is a lot," Ridley replied. "My mom followed the try for a girl route."

"Is that route typical?" Estella asked.

"Kinda, but there isn't usually a strategy to it. We just take life as it comes and at the end of the day count our blessings," Ridley replied.

"That's kind of how my family was," Estella stated, "if you add begging and praying for another day of being alive to the mix."

"I'm afraid to ask," Ridley turned to face her.

"It's nothing," Estella said, turning away from him. She tried to ignore him, but she could feel his eyes staring at the back of her head.

"Fine." She faced him. "My parents never took risks and taught us never to take risks, because rabbits aren't lucky regardless of what anybody says. We stay in our lane because doing anything else is bound to fail. At the end of it all, no matter how safely you play it, you still die. I mean, look at my family." She made a sweeping gesture. "They played it safe their entire lives, and I'm still the only one left." She gave a big huff before falling back against the log. Ridley stared at her for a while before turning back toward the sky.

"This may be because I'm a fox, but I think you're taking a risk no other rabbit has ever made, and I think it's working." Estella shrugged her shoulders. "So, here's what I think. We continue doing what we're doing, and after winter, you can tell all the spring bunnies about the greatest festival of all time."

Estella gave something between a scoff and a sigh. "Might get them to take some risk, probably unnecessarily."

"No matter what we do, how well we plan it, or how good our intentions, there will always be risk. That's life," Ridley continued, staring up at the sky.

"I guess," She glanced at the fox beside her. Without thinking, she took his paw in hers. He said nothing. "That's life," she murmured.

Chapter 13

In the Light of Family

Ridley approached the clearing with his usual gunny sack and saw smoke rising from it. He grew cautious until he saw the masked rabbit stoking a fire in the middle of the glade. The fox began to saunter into the clearing as the masked rabbit looked up.

"Kit, I was wondering when you would show up," Estella said. She hadn't put her tail on yet but was wearing the mask as a precaution.

Even with it on lopsided, Ridley could tell she was smirking at him.

"Trying to roast marshmallows before the party?" Ridley asked.

"Just getting the cinders ready," Estella rolled her eyes under her mask.

"You would be if those were cedar branches," Ridley pointed to the fire. "You're burning birch."

Estella raised her mask. "It smelled like cedar when I collected it," she said, looking crestfallen.

"To a rabbit, maybe," Ridley doused the flames with the jug and started a new fire. He glanced over at the downcast rabbit. "It's one of the most common mistakes someone makes when learning. There'll be full grown foxes here tonight that won't know the difference."

"But we're not taking chances." She readjusted her mask.

"You've gotten good with ear wrappings," Ridley reassured her.

"They've gotten stiffer," Estella moaned. "And I think my snout's swelling up."

"It looks fine to me," Ridley reassured her.

The pair defaulted into their usual routine. Estella had no hesitation as Ridley marked her crown and neck. With a little help, she was able to fasten the faux tail around her waist. All that was left was the mask.

Estella rubbed the sides of her nose. "I still think it is swollen."

"Let me see," Ridley said. As soon as the rabbit took her hands away from her face, she bumped her nose with his before returning her mask to its usual place.

"I told you. You look fine." The fox shot her a cocky grin. Estella returned this display with a punch to the fox's arm.

"Easy, Cedar." Ridley rubbed his arm in mock pain. "Don't want to cause a kerfuffle."

Estella rolled her eyes under the mask as the pair made their way to the festival.

As the odd pair crossed the threshold, the rabbit noticed that the gathering had a much lower energy than the previous nights. Most foxes were sitting on nearby rocks and logs. A few were doing elaborate stretches. The banquet table had been reduced to mostly hors d'oeuvres and finger foods. The third bonfire hadn't even been lit yet.

"For a festival that was supposed to last a week, you guys seem to be crashing before the halfway point," Estella observed.

"That's something rabbits are known for," Ridley said, earning him a side eye glance from the masked rabbit. "Don't worry, the candle hasn't been lit yet."

The fox led the rabbit to the banquet table and started to fill two plates with fresh fruits and vegetables.

"Should we be eating this early?" Estella asked.

"Trust me, we'll need our energy tonight," Ridley replied.

"Riverbank Ridley!" a light brown fox sauntered over.

"In more ways than one," Ridley said under his breath.

The light brown fox threw his arm around Ridley's shoulders, "I have not seen you in ages. It's like you're avoiding me."

"I can't imagine why," Ridley replied sardonically.

The new light brown fox eyed the masked rabbit, "And who's this cute little vixen?"

"Cedar, this is my brother, Castor. Castor, this is Cedar," Ridley droned the introduction.

"Are you the one taking care of my little brother? He's sensitive you know," Castor remarked.

"I'm older and taller than you," Ridley replied, Castor's comments clearly getting under his skin.

"But you are sensitive," Castor said as he turned back to the masked rabbit. "Sorry if he's gotten touchy-feely with you. He's a big ole marshmallow."

"Cedar, do me a favor and take about three steps back," Ridley said expressionlessly. Cedar did as she was instructed. Ridley then took a grape from his plate and tossed it into the air.

"Grapes and quail!" he exclaimed. Ridley pretended to open his mouth to catch it as Castor made a move to snatch it from the air. Ridley then took this opportunity to put his brother in a headlock. The grape fell on the ground, forgotten.

"That's cheating!" Castor cried out.

"You were about to do the exact same thing to me, and don't pretend like you weren't," Ridley accused. The brothers continued to wrestle, with Ridley never surrendering the upper hand. Estella watched the display as she munched vegetables under her mask. Under duress, Castor soon tapped out and was released.

"Alright, now that we've got that out of the way..." Castor slammed down the drink closest to him. "Mom sent me to get you. We haven't seen you in forever."

Ridley hesitated, "I'm actually spending time with Ced..."

"Bring her too," Castor cut him off. He then grabbed his brother's arm and started dragging him away. Estella followed closely behind them.

Castor led the pair to a tall matronly vixen with sharp features, standing beside a vixen slightly younger than Estella and Ridley but with soft features identical to the older female. Upon seeing Ridley, the older vixen's face lit up.

"My kit finally returns," the matronly vixen smiled as she embraced Ridley.

"Hey, big brother," the younger vixen said. She and Ridley hugged as well.

"So good to see you guys," Ridley replied in earnest.

"You look thin! Have you been eating enough? Sleeping enough?" The mother vixen started to fret over her son.

"I never see you at the river anymore," the younger vixen said.

"It's a little too cold to swim," Ridley replied.

The older vixen turned to the masked rabbit. "And who's this?"

"Mom and Seren, this is my friend Ce..."

"Estella," the rabbit interrupted, extending her paw. "My friends call me Cedar."

"Nice to meet you, Estella." For half a second her eyes lit up. "I'm Celeste, mother of these untamed larrikins. I'm guessing you've met my rebellious sons, Ridley and Castor."

"Right. I'm the rebel of the family," Ridley said sardonically.

"Hey, I got hitched, so someone had to pick up my slack," Castor called.

"And this is my favorite daughter, Seren," Celeste finished.

"I'm her only daughter." Seren shook Estella's paw. "I love your tail by the way."

"Thanks. I've been working on it all day," Estella said.

"She's being modest. It looks like that naturally," Ridley remarked.

"Unlike you, Mr. Bushytail," Estella responded.

"Don't let the tail fool you. His teeth are sharp as are his claws," Castor not so subtly hinted at the masked rabbit.

"Shouldn't you be with your wife?" Ridley asked.

"Bailey took Ginger to be gushed and fawned over by her aunts. I swear they're planning on having all girls," Castor replied.

"I still can't believe you lived long enough to have children," Ridley remarked.

"For me the hard part was turning vixens away, the tall handsome tod that I am," Castor boasted.

"You married the first girl who smiled at you, and you know it."

"My girl has the best smile, and my lovely daughter has one to match. I'll show you sometime," Castor declared.

"As long as you're not talking, I'd love to," Ridley droned.

"Attention everyone!" a voice called. "Grab yourselves a plate and make your way to the center stage."

The odd pair merged into the wave with Ridley's fox family. Estella walked next to Seren and Ridley, trying unsuccessfully to avoid Castor. "I thought we blessed the food before everyone eats." Estella said.

"We do, but we're getting food now." Seren gave her a quizzical look. "Don't you remember?"

"My parents were stringent. This is my first festival. Ridley's been showing me everything there is to see," Estella replied. Seren smirked for half a second.

"Well, if there's anything you'd like to know, just ask me,"

"Thank you," Estella said.

"Just one question. Are you a good dancer?" His sister winked at Ridley.

After the vulpine had gathered, the meal was blessed, and everyone settled for the night. The Elder silver fox bellowed out, "For the dignity of all foxes, we must remember that honor must come before vanity. For vanity shall take more than it gives, and honor restores what might be lost..."

Chapter 14

Tail, Teeth, and Talon

There once were three foxes that would occasionally get together and argue that the finer points of their anatomy were not only the best among foxes, but the best a fox could have.

"It is clear that teeth are the best quality a fox can have," the first fox stated. "The sharpest fangs break the necks of our prey and cut the ties that would bind us. That is freedom and power, and it starts with the teeth."

"Respectfully, I disagree," said the second fox. "It is the claws that are the best. They hold down our prey to allow our precious fangs to work. It adds speed to our hunts and allows us access to the trees. That is security, speed, and the freedom you speak so highly about."

"Proper use of fangs render security a moot point, and it is the claws that get tangled," the first fox retorted.

"My fine not-so-furry friends, you are both wrong. Hunting is not life, but only a part of life. The majority will be spent at rest. In that sense, teeth and claws are less than useless. It is only the tail furry, bushy, beautiful, and warm, that aids us in this aspect. That is comfort and that is peace, not to mention our pride. That which makes us different from all other animals is the tail," the third fox gave his usual spiel.

The other foxes disagreed, and they argued. This was the norm for them each time they met.

The next time the foxes were to meet, the fox with sharp teeth arrived first, as usual. After waiting for a spell, the fox with a bushy tail arrived. Both foxes perked up their ears.

"Am I early?" the bushy-tailed fox asked. "I'm usually last." "Something's wrong." The fox with sharp teeth sniffed the air.

The foxes then heard the rattling of bells and a high-pitched bark. They sprinted towards the sound to find the fox with razor claws caught in a snare. The snare caused the bells to rattle every time she tugged. In the distance, they could hear barks and howls approaching.

"Get out of here," the trapped fox shouted.

"Not without you!" the fox with large teeth declared. "Hold still."

He grabbed the snare with his teeth and snapped it from the branch.

"Run!" he cried.

The three foxes ran as fast as their legs could carry them. Still, the barks and howls grew closer. The fox with razor claws stopped in front of a large tree.

"We can't outrun them," she shouted. She climbed about halfway up the trunk of the tree.

"Grab on to me and launch yourselves up," the fox with razor claws called to the others. They did as they were told, and the fox with razor claws followed until all three sat on a high branch.

"Get behind me," the fox with a bushy tail hissed. The others fell in behind him, and he used his tail to cover them all.

The barks and howls grew louder and stared at the trunk of the tree before passing and fading into the distance.

The foxes, not realizing they had been holding their breath, let out a sigh of relief. They all looked at each other, reflecting on their situation and the outcome.

"Let's agree to disagree from now on and never argue again," one of them proposed.

"Agreed!" the others stated.

Chapter 15

Dancing in the Dark

Once the Elder finished, the foxes in the clearing put down their plates and clapped. The Elder bowed slightly before addressing the audience once more. "I hope that the story left you all rested, refreshed, and reinvigorated because the dance marathon is about to begin!"

At that announcement, all the foxes stood up, disposed of their plates, and made their way to the dance clearing. The odd fox and rabbit duo were swept along with the crowd by the tod's family. Once the large group reached the clearing, the Elder stood before the band.

"Now, I know this festival is about coming together, but now comes the time to split y'all up! Everyone competing in the dance contest, grab your partner and move to my left. Everyone else, make your way to the right."

Tods and vixens began to move with their partners towards the group closest to the unlit fire pit. All the others passed by them, moving to join the other group.

"You and Estella going to try and win the dance marathon?" Castor asked his brother.

"You two should! It's not about dancing well. It's just endurance," Seren stated.

"Like I said, I'm not much of a dancer," Estella replied.

"Is everyone who's participating in the right group?" the Elder addressed the group to his right. They responded with nods and calls of yes. A few made last-minute preparations that they hoped would give them an edge.

The Elder looked across the entire crowd in front of him. "Now I need to tell you all not to be prideful." He scanned the crowd. "But I know what you want to do! You want to howl through your teeth, stomp your claws, and swish those BUSHY TAILS!" Cheers shot out from both sides. Foxes of all shapes and sizes hooped, hollered, and howled in excitement. Others stomped their feet, clapped their paws, and wagged their tails with anticipation.

"For those of you who are new or need reminders, the rules are simple. Once the sun has disappeared from the sky, we light the fire. I yell 'go'. The marathon begins. It will not end until the sun comes back up, and only one couple remains. There can only be one pair of winners, and they must keep dancing 'til the sun rises anew. Your partner can be anyone: your brother, sister, cousin, best friend, spouse, or someone you just met. Remember, you cannot trade partners at any point after the contest has started. So, if you want to switch, now's the time."

Tods and vixens held each other's paws and exchanged reassuring glances and smiles. Brothers clapped each other on their shoulders and nodded at others while faces beamed. Sisters wagged their tails and jumped up and down in anticipation. A few lone stragglers decided to quit early and made their way to the other group. One nervous-looking tod scanned the group of participants as if looking for a different partner. The vixen beside him grasped his paw tightly and shook her head at him. There was a couple toward the back, significantly older than the rest of the participants. The older tod wrapped his arm around the vixen's waist. "I think I'll pick you," he said to her. She blushed at the well-worn pick-up line as she did every time he said it.

"Sadly, everyone will leave empty-handed except the pair that outlasts the others. They —" he paused for dramatic effect, "will have their names carved into the Stone of Eternity!"

The Elder gestured to a large flat stone held up by a muscled fox. It was then that the rabbit noticed that similar stones surrounded the unlit pit, the only pit to have them.

"Their stone and their names will join the stones of former champions and be remembered from now until the end of time itself!" the Elder declared. The crowds cheered, excitement and nervous energy pouring out of them.

"Now then," the Elder grabbed a torch and raised it high above him. "Without further ado…." He hurled the torch into the center of the fire pit. Fire erupted, and soon the blaze was towering over the festival.

"BEGIN!" the Elder declared.

The band exploded into fast-paced euphoric music, and foxes from all sides started dancing. The odd pair and the fox's family stood back as the dance clearing was transformed. Vulpine of all kinds moved their bodies in a rhythmic chaos. Eyes roamed from a vixen kicking and her paws never touching the ground to watching a tod doing a no-paws backhand spring. Partners were tossed into the air as the music pulsed, only to be caught, dipped, and twirled as if they weighed nothing. Leaps, bounds, and movements that seemed impossible became the norm.

The pandemonium proceeded through a fifteen-minute song, and then the music stalled for a slight moment while the tempo changed. Several foxes filtered out as the music turned from upbeat and chaotic to strong and steady. The dancing itself became more measured as those who remained traded the impromptu acrobatics for what the rabbit recognized as dancing. The marathoners were still going strong as the elderly couple strolled out, the vixen clearly having had enough dancing for the night.

"Well, I'm off to find my dance partner," Castor said. "Don't be too surprised when we amaze you. We're old pros at this."

As he walked away, he addressed the odd couple. "Remember to make room for modesty, you two." He winked at his brother. Ridley shot him an annoyed glance. Estella turned her head away.

"Ignore him," Seren addressed Estella. "Blocking him out took years of practice, but you get better at it."

"Be nice to your brother. So far, he's the only one of you who's settled down, not to mention started a family," Celeste addressed her progeny.

"It's much easier to be nice to him when he's not here," Ridley stated.

"True," Celeste relented.

The group continued to watch the dance unfold as foxes of all shapes, sizes, colors, and ages filtered in and out of the dance floor. The dancing itself ranged from rehearsed professional to talented fun to basic learning to children poorly imitating something unidentifiable.

Marathoners soon began dropping out, either growing tired, hurting their paws, or just losing interest.

After a while, the Elder stepped up to the stage to address the crowd. "Alright, I think it's time to give those in the marathon a little break. They can't stop, but we can slow the music down." On cue, the music slowed into a foxtrot. "Now would also be a great time to grab that special someone and show them just how special they are!"

The marathoners slowed their movements to match the music. Partners got into proper stances, while other pairs danced on their own. A pair of brothers begin dancing slowly in a manner that was either a bad interpretive dance or them trying to command the plants between them to grow. On the other side of the dance floor, foxes of all kinds were leading their partners and swaying to the music.

"You two should go!" Seren exclaimed to the odd pair.

"We don't… I don't…." Ridley stammered.

"Sure," Estella said, holding out her paw to Ridley. Astonished, Ridley took her paw and followed the masked rabbit. A nice-looking tod asked Seren if she would like to dance. She looked back at her mother who gave a silent nod of approval.

A vixen no older than Seren stood before the band holding a string instrument. Her voice was powerful, as it carried through the clearing. The dark, warm melodies enchanted the dancers, and it felt like a cozy warm blanket had been laid over the festival.

"I feel myself rising — My feet spinning on the air"

The fox inhaled at the top of the masked rabbit's crown. Cedar filled his nostrils. Ridley peered over Estella's head at the hordes of vulpine surrounding them. He searched for prying eyes, curious inhales, or anyone who looked at the odd pair just a little too long. To his surprise, nobody even glanced in their direction.

Most had their eyes closed as they held and were held in the arms and tails of their partner. Those with their eyes open were looking like the person across from them was the only person in the world. He looked over at his sister, and she couldn't stop smiling. He looked over at his brother, holding a blooming vixen that looked like she had just opened her eyes last week. Ginger. She giggled as her father lifted her up over his head and brought her down into a barrage of kisses.

Ridley looked at the girl in front of him. She smiled at him through her eyes and swayed like a flower petal on a breeze. She gave him a comforting squeeze before relaxing into his embrace. For the first time in the fox's life, he truly did feel as if he were floating off the ground and nothing could touch him. He decided to do the one thing he'd never done. He held the girl in front of him, closed his eyes, and just breathed.

"I left earth behind... for the stars in your eyes"

After a while, the band picked back up into full swing. The odd pair made their way discreetly back to the tod's mother who was waiting for them.

"You're not going to keep dancing?" Celeste asked the younger pair.

"We're not much for dancing," Ridley replied. Estella nodded in agreement.

"Could have fooled me," Celeste smirked at them.

As the night wore on, the marathoners slowed to a constant pace. Fatigue set in, and couples randomly began to drop out. The non marathoners had broken into groups. Old and young couples danced with each other, trying to regain that warm, raising, glowing feeling of new and powerful love. Some were feeling it for the first time.

Adolescents grouped together to show off moves they had "invented." Parents and grandparents gathered around to watch their kits dance by themselves.

The music slowed down once more, and Ridley ghosted a glance at Estella with a question on the tip of his tongue when—

"Excuse me, ma'am," a young kit walked up to the masked rabbit. "May I have this dance?"

Estella's eye lit up. "Of course, young gentleman." She presented her paw, and the kit took it.

"Take care of her for me," Ridley told the young tod as he led her to the dance floor. They danced at arm's length as Estella followed the tod's unsure lead. He kept looking down at the ground to make sure he wouldn't step on her feet, and Estella encouraged him and dipped under his spins.

"She's good with kids," Celeste stated, giving her son a not-so-subtle side eye.

"I guess so," Ridley answered, not liking where the conversation was heading.

"Did you know I almost named you Sirius?" Celeste declared.

"I did not know that," Ridley answered, though given the star theme of his siblings, he wasn't too surprised.

Celeste faced her son in full. "I know why you told everyone her name was Cedar."

Ridley's heart went into his throat. "You do?"

"Oh course," she gave him a sly smile. "You didn't want me knowing her name was Estella."

Ridley's heart went back into his chest as he wore a confused expression. "Why would I do that?"

"You didn't want your mother interfering with your love life," Celeste huffed. "I'm a little taken aback, to be honest."

"That was not the reason," Ridley defended himself.

"Oh, please, you can't lie to your mother. I see the way you look at her, the way you smile at her when she's not looking, and you've been happier with her than I've seen you in a long time."

"I...I...I," Ridley stammered, trying to think of an excuse or an explanation.

"Don't worry, I won't get in your way. Besides," Celeste said looking up, "I'm the night sky. I could always use another star."

Ridley turned red as a beet and didn't respond. He kept his eyes glued to Estelle as the band wrapped up the song. She and her young dance partner made their way back to the small group.

"Thank you, ma'am! You're unbelievably beautiful," the young tod complimented her.

"Thank you, and you're quite handsome yourself," Estella said.

The young fox beamed.

"Thanks for showing my date how to dance," Ridley smiled at the young tod.

"Thank you, sir," the young fox awkwardly bowed to them both before hurrying away.

"Well, I'll just leave you two," Celeste said, wrapping her son in a hug. When she pulled away, she raised her finger at him. "You better be a gentleman."

"I will," Ridley promised.

"Good," Celeste walked over to Estella. "It was so great to meet you, Estella." She wrapped the masked rabbit in her arms before whispering in her ear. "Scratch him behind his left ear, and he's yours." She then broke the hug, walked off, and disappeared into the crowd.

"I like your mom," Estella said as she and Ridley made their way away from the festival. It was barely the crack of dawn as the first specks of light peaked over the horizon. A few brave souls still tried to win the dance marathon, long since trading any semblance of rhythm for the barest definition of movement.

"Yeah, she can be a handful," Ridley admitted.

"Still, the formal dancing and meeting your parents has been nice," Estella said, looking down at the ground. Ridley gave her a quizzical look.

"Don't rabbits do any of that?" he asked.

"Not in the slightest. The whole idea of romance is vague in rabbit terms. Sure, there's the idea of meeting *the one* and falling in love, but otherwise, there's only it'll happen when it happens, and you'll know when you know," Estella stated.

"I have a feeling your parents told you that a lot," Ridley observed.

"They did," Estella admitted. "You know I never knew how my parents met or why they loved each other, but I know they did." She nodded her head. "I'm sure of it."

"As am I," Ridley concluded.

"What about foxes? Romance seems to come easy, but where does love come in?" Estella asked.

Ridley thought for a moment. "Well, you're right that romance comes second nature to us," Ridley stated. "Love, however, is trickier. It's multi-faceted. It exists in many forms—romantic, familial, divine. We tell our stories to try and make sense of it, but we'll never truly understand it. The one thing I know for certain, however, is that love is and will forever be the best thing we do."

"I always felt actions were the most important aspect," Estella stated.

Ridley glanced at her, "Come to my den."

"What?" Estella blinked back in surprise.

"Everyone always skips the fourth or fifth nights because they're too tired. I was going to skip tomorrow so you should come to my den."

"Ummmm...." Estella hesitated.

"It's okay if you don't." Ridley looked away.

"No—okay," Estella stammered. "I'll come."

Ridley smiled, "Great."

"Where is it?" Estella asked.

"I'm going there now, so I'll show you."

Ridley continued to lead the masked rabbit to the side of a hill with an old apple tree on top. He cleared away a pile of brush to reveal a wooden door the same color as the ground.

"This is my place." He turned to the rabbit. "I was about to turn in."

"Did you want to—come inside?" he inquired.

"No—that's fine," Estella stammered. "But, I'll see you tomorrow."

"Great," Ridley said. "I'll see you then."

Estella walked away slowly. She paused for a moment and shook her head. When she took off her mask, Ridley saw the blush on her cheeks.

Chapter 16

Blood Red Soup and Unwelcome Guests

This is crazy. This is crazy. This is crazy. Estella shook her head as she walked up to the fox's den. She knocked and adjusted her mask. After a few seconds, Ridley opened the door. He smiled at the sight of her.

"You came," he declared. "Come in. It's cold outside." He ushered her in.

Estella looked around the cozy fox den. The den had a modest-sized fireplace with a full chimney and two large stacks of firewood on either side. A cast-iron pot hung on a swivel, heating over the fire. There was a small kitchen nook with several cupboards and a water basin. Cushions lined the fireplace, and the largest one sat in the middle of a nest of leaves on the right side of the hobble. The left side housed half a dozen wooden barrels and a bookshelf.

"Make yourself at home," Ridley welcomed.

"Thank you." Estella warmed her paws by the fire. Ridley walked over to the barrels.

"Water or cider?"

"Water's fine," she answered. She looked at the pot hanging over the fire. A gnawing feeling in the back of her head led her to wonder was inside it. An old instinct told her to run. Instead, she stayed and hoped Ridley didn't see her worry through the mask.

Ridley brought her water and made his way to the kitchen. He returned with two bowls. Estella sipped her water under her mask.

"Why are you in your getup? I told you we're not going tonight," Ridley said.

"I thought you might change your mind, or someone might see me come in," Estella answered.

"Well, I appreciate the foresight, but you should take off the mask. I want to see your face when you see the surprise." A grin lit up Ridley's face. "I just hope the cast-iron pot didn't give it away." Ridley slowed down as he noticed no bubbling sound from his surprise. "I was here all day, and I forgot to put the cast iron on sooner," Ridley shook his head.

"It's alright," Estella put her paw on his shoulder. She had no idea what was bothering him and was a little afraid to ask, but she rubbed his back in reassurance.

"You're right," Ridley swallowed. "It doesn't take away from the main surprise." He reached over and, with a flourish, removed the top of the pot.

"Voila," he exclaimed. The pot revealed a light red, almost orange liquid. The warm, heavenly aroma of tomatoes and carrots filled her nostrils. Her eyes lit up, but Ridley's face fell.

"Darn it," he muttered.

"What's wrong?" Estella asked.

"It's supposed to be vegetable stew," Ridley sighed. "I must have added too much water or not enough milk or..."

"I bet it's delicious," Estella cut him off.

"One way to find out." Ridley dipped the bowls into the pot. They said grace and took a sip from their bowls. At least, Estella tried to sip from hers, but her mask got in the way. Chuckling, she placed her mask to the side and took a proper sip of the soup. It tasted as good as it smelled. The rich, earthy flavor mixed with the zing of the tomatoes and a sweetness she couldn't identify. The flavors combined and ended with a kick of spice. It warmed her from the inside out.

"How is it?" Ridley stammered.

"Delicious." Estella was delighted with the dish. Ridley's downcast look transformed into a wide-brim smile.

"I'm glad you like it," he said. "I added extra carrots." Now Estella couldn't hide a smile. "I just wish I'd remembered to cook the bread."

"I think it's perfect." She took another sip. "And it's tangy." Estella raised her bowl towards her fox host. "Cheers."

"Cheers!" Ridley clinked their bowls together.

Halfway through their second bowls, Estella asked, "So how did you find this place?"

"I don't like talking about it," Ridley said. He would not look at her.

"Come on," Estella pleaded, "It's not embarrassing, is it?"

"No, but it might put a damper on things," Ridley stated.

"Come on, I'm a big girl," Estella insisted.

Ridley sighed. "You know the apple tree at the top of the hill?" Estella nodded her head. "That's how I met the Groves, a couple of black and white badgers who used to own this place. During the apple-picking season, Mr. Grove recruited this other beaver kit, Harry and me, to haul apples for him. He paid us with a bushel each."

"He didn't have cubs of his own?" Estella asked.

"Two girls, but the mother wouldn't let them lift a finger," Ridley said.

"Anyway, when the girls grew up, they got married and moved too far away for the Groves to visit. Mr. Groves got so old that I was doing most of the picking myself."

"What about Harry?" Estella asked.

"I haven't seen him since we were both kits. I hope he's doing alright." Ridley's eyes lost focus as they glazed over.

"Mrs. Groves showed me the recipe for her homemade cider, and it was the best I'd ever had. Beats the stuff they serve at the festival, and that's the truth. I still have a barrel saved for special occasions." He pointed to a barrel in the corner of the room. "I've tried, but I can't get it just right." Ridley's face fell. "I thought she was doing it to be nice or grateful, but then I realized that without me, she had nobody to teach. She and Mr. Groves were here alone. When she died, Mr. Groves told me he didn't want to hang around without her."

Estella's smile faded, and she felt a tear trace down her cheek.

"He said I could have the place on one condition after he was gone. I must bury him under a live oak tree. He's buried right out there." Ridley pointed out the door. "First thing I see when I walk out." He looked around the room. "I've made this place my own, but I honestly didn't change it much. I still sometimes get the feeling that I'm going to come in and see them, like they never left."

Estella put down her bowl. They had eaten nearly four bowls each as he had told the story. Now she reached over and placed her paw on the fox's shoulder. Ridley slowly refocused his eyes on her. Neither noticed that they were leaning towards each other.

THUMP THUMP THUMP. Someone knocked loudly on the door. They tensed.

"Were you expecting anybody else?" Estella asked.

"No." Ridley swallowed. His expression then went from alert to relaxed. "It's probably Castor."

"Your brother?" Estella let out a breath.

"Yeah, which means he either wants me to come to the festival with him, or he brought some cider and wants to drink with me. Either way, you should put your mask back on," Ridley instructed. Estella did as she was told.

"What if he wants to come in?" she asked.

"Then let's hope he brought three glasses." Ridley smiled as he made his way to the door. When he opened the door, he immediately frowned.

"Hey, handsome." A voice rang through the house.

"Jazz, what are you doing here?" Ridley wore a puzzled expression.

"I thought you could use some company." The vixen waltzed in without waiting to be invited. "Didn't want you cooped up here by yourself...." She stopped and turned around when she spotted Estella.

"What's she doing here?" Jazz demanded.

"I invited her," Ridley replied, "and I don't remember inviting you."

Jazz turned back to the masked rabbit. She scrunched up her face as though she smelled a dead, rotten fish. "Cedar, was it?"

"My friends call me Cedar. You can call me Estella," Her annoyance clearly shown. Jazz tilted her head at the masked rabbit.

"Why are you still wearing that mask?" she asked, her voice dripping in condescension. Ridley was about to speak when Estella cut him off.

"Because I look good. It's called self-respect. You should try it sometime." The temperature in the room dropped twenty degrees.

"While I'm all for being festive, I know that persons who wear masks typically aren't much to look at," Jazz snarked.

"For the record, I've seen Estella without her mask, and she looks better than you do every day of the week." Ridley moved to stand next to Estella.

"So, she's Estella. I thought you were friends," Jazz mocked.

"I like the way he says it," Estella retorted, "and he says it a lot."

Jazz looked from Ridley to Estella and back again. Estella gravitated towards the larger fox. Ridley's tail reached for Estella's midsection. Neither was looking at Jazz with much patience or kindness. The vixen decided to put her cards on the table.

"Come on, Ridley. You've known this girl how long? Less than a week? We've known each other all our lives. I know you. And you know me," she implored. "What do you know about her? Some shut-in who gave herself to the first guy who gave her attention? You can do so much better."

Ridley glared at her, fire in his eyes. "First, I didn't invite you. You came in without permission. Second, Estella has shown herself to be better than most people I've met in my life. Third, I do know you, and I can frankly say I've never been interested. If you think that I would be, especially with you coming in and insulting my guests, you clearly don't know me at all. And lastly, I didn't invite you in! Please leave!"

Jazz shrank back but quickly recovered. "Fine," she said, "I'll leave you two *freaks* be." She turned and headed for the door.

"Wait!" Estella called to her. "Before you go, make sure you tell whoever you end up with that they were your second choice." Estella glared at her, the mask doing little to hide the somber disapproval.

"Like you were my first choice," Jazz spat back at Ridley.

"That sounds like you get rejected a lot," Ridley said.

Jazz opened her mouth and then closed it. She then turned and left in a huff.

Estella's expression turned smug as the vixen tramped out of the burrow. She turned to see Ridley with a sly brim smile.

"What?" she asked.

"You stood your ground with her," Ridley stated.

"To be fair, she wasn't very witty," Estella said.

"But you didn't run or try to get out of the fray. You fought." Ridley's smile grew wider, showing off his teeth. Estella looked away.

"It was nothing," she stammered.

"If you say so." He returned to the fireplace. "I'm going to refill our drinks," Ridley hurried to the barrels in the corner of the room. He didn't know she was blushing under her mask.

Chapter 17
The Hungry Wolf and Heaven's Reflections

hat story did the Elder tell this night?" Estella asked. The two had retired for the evening and were sharing the large bed in the corner of the room. Ridley had insisted that she take it herself, and Estella had suggested they share it. She had also gotten comfortable, removing her mask and bindings. They were now stretched on their backs, lying next to each other, and staring at the den's ceiling.

"I'm not sure I could do it justice," Ridley replied.

"Do it anyway." Stella flicked her ears, "I'm all ears."

Ridley chuckled. "Well, bear with me."

"There once was a fox who looked at his place in the world. Some animals were smaller, but also ones that were much larger. His survival depended not on his speed and strength but on his cunning. Even then, he would have to bow to forces stronger than he was. The fox decided he didn't like that. He decided that the only way he could matter in this world was to become bigger than the forces that opposed him. Or else he would be nothing.

"He hunted and gathered all he could and ate until he was big enough. Then he turned to larger prey. He continued this routine until he was about the size of a wolf. Then winter came. The fox promised himself that when spring returned, he would continue his undertaking until he was the size of a bear. Then no force could stand against him.

When the fox emerged thinner in the spring, he returned to his old hunting grounds. Rather than find the bustle of new life, he found everything bare. The bushes that gave him berries had been stripped clean. The scurrying of mice and smaller animals had been silenced. The ripple of swimming fish was replaced with still water. The fox searched far and wide, only to find nothing to nourish him.

He returned to the water to drink until he became too weak to leave. Only then, he realized that nothing survived as he had taken everything last year.

As he lay dying, he thought, "Nothing stands against me because there was nothing left."

"Wow," was all Estella could think to say.

"Yeah," Ripley sighed. "The Elder would always talk about how the story meant there was a time to hunt and a time to let be, a time to act and a time to rest, a time to mourn and a time to dance, and how now was a time to dance." Ridley smiled.

"I think now is the time for rest," Estella said.

"I couldn't agree more."

The fox snuggled into his bed, closed his eyes, and breathed slowly. Shortly, he slept. The rabbit, however, couldn't keep her eyes closed. Far from uncomfortable, her mind raced, refusing to let Estella stay calm for more than a few seconds. Her musings had nothing and everything to do with the fox beside her and the story he had just told.

Leaning over, she shook the fox's shoulder. "Hmm," he grunted, blinking his eyes open. "Do you think there's a heaven?"

The fox lifted himself in a stretch. He focused his eyes on her. "I like to think so. Why do you ask?"

The rabbit turned to face the ceiling. "It's just—watching my family die, and now they're just gone—it's a lot to process," Estella paused. "After it happened, I didn't think I would live much longer, so grieving, planning, or just trying to make sense of it all didn't seem important. Now it's all I can think about. Most days, I feel like my head's going to burst."

Ridley placed a comforting paw on her shoulder. "Just talk it out.

"Will that work?" Estella asked.

"It's a start."

Estella took a deep breath, "The idea that there's something more than this life feels insulting, like everything's just going to be okay after we die. Is there a realm of endless peace after a lifetime of suffering? Then why have the suffering in the first place? To placate a mistake somebody else made? To act like everyone who dies goes to some better place makes it seem like they didn't matter. But if I reject the idea, there's no alternative. They're all just gone, and then it's like they never mattered — like they never even existed, or like I don't matter and if I die, it'll be like I was never here. What's the point of life if it ends?" The rabbit finally let herself breathe, feeling relieved, anxious, energized, and exhausted at the same time. She turned away from the fox, curled up, and withdrew into herself.

Ridley moved closer and wrapped his arm around her waist and his tail around her body.

"I'm not trying to be selfish," Estella stated.

"I know you're not."

He pulled her closer and leaned into her ears. "My father once asked me, 'Can you believe there's a Heaven, if you don't believe there's a Hell?' I answered that you must believe in both. Your choices, how you treat people, and how you live your life all must mean something. If that means there's a right and a wrong, I'm willing to have a little faith."

"Still, you think there's something just beyond what we can see?" Estella asked.

"Have you ever read a book?"

"I've read a few."

"Do you know what happens when a book ends?"

"No," Estella responded.

"You read the next one," Ridley stated. "When one story ends, another one begins, at least that's how I like to see things."

Estella further relaxed into Ridley's embrace. After a moment, she turned to face him.

"Am I a coward?" she asked.

Ridley couldn't help but smirk. "So says the rabbit in the fox's den."

"No, it was that when danger came, I ran. I couldn't save any of them. When it mattered, I just couldn't…," Estella's voice faded.

Ridley pulled her close. "Sometimes in life you must save yourself, and that's more than enough. If you didn't contribute to someone's downfall to save or benefit yourself, then you're not a coward." Ridley shook his head. "If you can save others, that's great, but sometimes the hero you've been waiting for has to be you. And if the only person you end up saving in this life is yourself, you're still the hero."

Estella wrapped her arm around Ridley's waist and buried her head in his chest.

"Are you saving me?" she mumbled into his chest. "Do you need saving?"

"I don't know." The pair remained in their silent embrace until Estella's mind finally let her eyes close. After several moments, she was asleep, breathing lightly with her chest rising and falling.

Ridley took the opportunity to lean his mouth closer to her head. He whispered in her ear, "Wanna hear a secret? You're the one saving me. At least that's how I see things." Ridley kissed the top of her head. He then placed the bottom of his head on top of hers. Sleep found him soon after.

Chapter 18

One Time, One Line

The newly awakened fox looked at the rabbit he had met only five days ago. Had it only been five? It felt like a lifetime ago. He looked at her as though he was seeing her for the first time. Her little cotton tail seemed fluffier, and her ears looked a little shorter. Had they always been pointed? It might have been just the remnants of the ribbon wrap. She still had the brushing of cedar ash gracing her head and neck. Otherwise, she was the same rabbit he'd met five days ago. Wait—the eyes—they've changed. More determined? No, same beautiful blue eyes he saw that day, same ones that made him talk to her to begin with. Without waking the beauty beside him, he rose and made his way to the kitchen area.

Later, when a pleasant redolent scent filled the den, the aroma woke her from slumber. She scanned the area around her for a second to remember where she was. She smiled once she saw her fox by the fire. He moved the caldron holding the leftover soup to the back of the fire and placed a covered cast-iron skillet and a tea kettle at the front.

Estella made her way to the fire as the fox noticed and smirked at her.

"Morning, sleepyhead," he greeted.

"Have I overslept? I regret nothing." Estella said. "I haven't slept that well in the longest while."

"I'm glad. What do you like?"

She gave him a confused look.

"Tea," the fox clarified. "Black, mint? Prefer chamomile myself."

"Do you have jasmine?" the rabbit asked.

"Of course, you'd pick that one." The fox shook his head with a smirk.

"What?"

"That stuff tastes like grass," Ridley declared.

"It tastes like flowers."

"Call it what you want, it's still bitter."

"That's only if you scald it," Estella defended. "I can see why they still call you Kit."

The fox shook his head as he added the jasmine and water to both cups and handed one to the rabbit. She waited before sipping hers.

"Making biscuits?" Estella nodded toward the cast-iron skillet.

"Better," Ridley removed the lid with a flourish. The dish appeared to be cornbread, but a darker shade. The fox cut his friend a slice. The smell was intoxicating. She took a bite.

Ridley watched Estella's eyes light up as the warm bread with the faint taste of cinnamon enveloped her taste buds. "It's — `sweet. Like carrot cake, but not quite."

"You're close. It's pumpkin bread," Ridley said. "You've never had it before?"

The rabbit shook her head. "Pumpkins didn't last long in our house. If we were lucky, a bunch of the older siblings and our father would carry a pumpkin from wherever it was growing to our burrow, and our mother would turn the pumpkin into its own cauldron of pumpkin soup."

"An edible cauldron?"

"When you're young, you get the soup, and once you're older, you get a piece of the pumpkin." She dipped her bread into her tea. "It's not nearly as good as this, though."

"Given your place in the pecking order, I'm guessing you didn't usually get the best pick."

"Almost never!" Estella stated. "If I got any treats at all, they were stale." Ridley wordlessly gave her another piece. "Outside of this, I've only had one fresh treat in my life. My aunt saved me a fresh yeast cookie with sugar frosting once. Best I've ever had." She looked down at her piece of pumpkin bread. "Present dish excluded."

"I'd imagine it's a little rough growing up with such a big family in a single burrow," the fox observed.

"It wasn't all bad. The winter holidays were the best! Since most of my family was white or light gray, we could go out into the snow without being scared. Whenever the first heavy snow fell, we'd all run outside and play. There was sledding, having snowball fights, and sliding on the ice."

"I can't imagine sliding on the ice being fun with multiple bodies."

"It was necessary when a sibling slid out too far. We linked together to pull him back in," Estella clarified.

Ridley chuckled. "That would have been fun to watch."

"Only fun if you watch?" Estella shook her head. "We'd also make giant snow bunnies."

"Snow bunnies?"

"Yes, giant snow bunnies with ears, a cottontail, and shining rocks for the eyes and nose. When our bunny was complete, their head would be as big as our dad! Maybe bigger," Estella exclaimed.

Ridley wore a perplexed look on his face. "That explains--so much."

"What?"

"When I was a foxling, really young," Ridley clarified, "I found a snow bunny like you're describing, but I thought it was real."

"You thought a rabbit was that big?"

"Yeah, when I got close, I noticed it wasn't moving. I thought the cold got to it."

"You didn't notice that his ears, tail, and everything else was made of snow?" Estella asked.

"I thought that's what happened when animals froze to death. The sight of the frozen bunny made me sad." He looked to see Estella snicker at him. "I was young!" he exclaimed.

"You don't have to tell me." She snickered even harder. "You big ole softy."

Ridley rolled his eyes.

"But once we were done or the pads of our paws froze," Estella continued, "we'd all come in for hot tea, cookies, and warm blankets, and then just cuddle up together." She smiled. She turned back to her fox. "What about you? Do you like the winter holidays?"

"Hate to disappoint, but I've always been a summer fox." Ridley replied. "It was the best time to swim."

"Should have known, Mr. Riverbank Ridley." Estella smiled slyly.

"You should have seen me in my prime. Foxes from all over would come to the special branch with the logger's rope. We would all see who could swing out the farthest, who could make the biggest splash, and who could do the most flips. I had them all beat."

Ridley got a far-off look in his eyes. "The sunset was the best part. When the light created a bridge across the water, I felt like it was calling me to walk across. I and so many others, before and after me, attempted it too, but," he shook his head, "it never did work." Estella smiled.

"There was this one night when Castor, our cousin, Oz, and I stayed up all night by the river."

"All night?"

"Yeah. After a full day of swimming, we stayed on the riverbank. We lit a campfire, caught some fish, roasted them, and watched the night sky light up." He chuckled. "I had brought a jug of cider that the Groves gave to me. I would always hide it from Castor, so he could never find it. Anyway, I pulled it out and passed it around. Then we started singing every song we knew at the top of our lungs, not a care in the world."

Estella gave him a warm smile. "Sounds fun."

"It was. Then, when we ran out of songs, we told ghost stories. We kept trying to scare each other, but it never worked. The three of us thought we were invincible. If we stuck together, we could've taken on a mountain lion if we wanted." Ridley lifted his glass in the air as if ready to go on his next noble quest.

"Where has Oz gone?" Estella asked. "I don't think I've seen him at the festival."

Ridley's mood deflated, his eyes turned downcast once more, "I haven't seen him for a while."

"Do you know where he is? Or do you know someone who might?"

"I don't know," the fox responded.

Estella's face fell, "You guys seemed close."

"We only stayed at the river that one time," Ridley clarified. "We always meant to do it again, or something like it, but we never did."

Estella's face went from sad to perplexed. "I don't get what's up with you and your brother. You seem to want nothing to do with him, but you were expecting him last night. Are you guys close or not?"

"That night I told you about was a fluke or a miracle, whatever you want to call it. In our early adolescence, we were all a little reckless. The difference between Castor and me was that I didn't know how to start, and he didn't know when to stop. Since I was the oldest, I was always the one bailing him out. It got worse when our dad died. He stopped listening to me or our mom. He would probably be dead if he hadn't met Bailey."

"But he got better, didn't he?" Estella asked.

"He's never apologized for what he put us through or even admitted he'd done anything wrong. He acts like he can just show up in our lives like nothing happened. Our mom says we should forgive him, but I struggle with it."

"Still, maybe a cup of cider between you two could patch things up?" Estella smiled optimistically.

Ridley returned her smile with a sad one of his own, "Castor's always wanted a drinking buddy, and we both knew from the start that it was never going to be me."

Estella remained silent for a while. Finally, she said, "You're never going to remake things the way they were, but you can always create something new."

"Words to live by." He then refilled their cup, and they toasted once more.

Chapter 19

Sugar and Ginger

The odd pair made their way from the clearing after their now usual routine of applying cedar cinders to the masked rabbit.

"You know, I wouldn't have minded staying in tonight. The soup and some cornbread would have been more than enough," Estella commented.

Ridley smirked, "A snow bunny like yourself should know that come winter, soup and bread are the only things to eat. Now's the only time to get some bulk and variety."

"Compared to what I usually eat, your cooking *is* bulk and variety," Estella said with no hints of sadness in her voice. She winked at Ridley.

Unconsciously, Ridley smiled back. "Still let's taste what tonight has to offer."

"Lead the way," The pair crossed the threshold once more.

The congregation of vulpine must have followed the odd pair's lead as all the attendees had become invigorated and determined to finish the rest of the festival strongly. The Elder fox had to shout over the pulsating noise to make his usual announcement. After the meal was blessed, vulpine of all kinds made their way to the buffet table.

The odd pair broke towards opposite sides with Estella in line behind a red, curvy vixen. When they reached the end, the vixen began bouncing between the fresh fruit and fruit-based desserts.

"Sorry," the vixen apologized. "I haven't had sugar in the longest time. My pregnancy drove my sweet tooth nuts, and now I finally get to have some."

"Don't let me stop you," Estella said.

"Here!" the vixen offered Estella the last slice of pineapple upside down cake. Estella politely declined as the vixen added the slice to her plate. The masked rabbit then offered her the best grapes she could find, which the vixen gratefully accepted.

"Grapes and quail!" Estella exclaimed.

"Grapes and quail!" the vixen chorused.

"Grapes and quail!" Ridley echoed from his side of the table.

The vixen looked up. "Ridley, is that you?"

Recognition washed over the tod's face, "Bailey, I didn't notice you."

The vixen placed her food at the end of the table, and the two foxes briefly embraced. "It's good to see you."

"Are you sure?" Bailey asked. "I haven't lost my figure, have I?"

"Come spring, we'll all be skin and bones, so it's best to eat now and worry about figures later," Ridley reassured her.]

"Don't listen to him. He's been trying to fatten me up all week," Estella interjected.

"I'm sorry," Ridley stated. "Estella, this is my brother's wife, Bailey. Bailey, this is my good friend, Estella."

Bailey beamed, "You're Estella? Castor told me all about you! I knew there was something I liked about you." She swept Estella into a hug as if they were old friends. Estella was stunned at first but returned her warm embrace.

Bailey beamed as she stepped back. "Ridley, you need to come with me and meet your niece!"

"I was there when she was born," Ridley said.

"But she hasn't seen you yet. She just opened her eyes." She turned to Estella, "And she'll have to meet this cutie!"

Estella gave a small smile under her mask. "I hear she has a great smile."

Bailey's face lit up. "The very best." She led the odd pair away from the table, piled high with desserts in her hand.

As they walked, Ridley gave out a low whistle. The masked rabbit peeked at him as he handed her a small parcel wrapped in a napkin. She opened it to find four fresh yeast cookies with sugar frosting. She beamed under her mask in a way only her fox could tell.

The odd pair followed Bailey to a group of vixens surrounding a single tod, who held a newborn foxling in his arms. He was making a game of causing her to giggle, which she seemed to enjoy. Of the vixens, one had a daughter born in the springtime who was clearly still getting used to no longer being the center of attention. Another was noticeably pregnant and being supported by her sister, who was neither showing nor had any children with her.

Castor saw his mate approach with his brother and Cedar, and his face lit up even more. "Ridley!" He turned to the vixen in his arms. "Precious, it's your Uncle Ridley. Say hi." The tiny vixen squeaked a greeting at the new tod.

Ridley took the vixen into his arms as if he had done it a thousand times. The vixen smiled at the attention she received from her soon-to-be favorite uncle. Bailey shot Estella a knowing look, which left her embarrassed, but unable to stop smiling.

"Estella, I'd like you to meet my sisters." She indicated the vixen with her daughter. "This is Ann and her daughter, Annie."

"Nice to meet you," Ann said.

"Hey," Annie muttered.

"The pleasure's mine." Estella leaned down. "I must say, you're the best-looking vixen I've seen all night."

"You're just saying that." Annie turned away, failing to hide a smile.

"Annie, we say thank you when someone compliments us," her mother scolded.

"Thank you, Miss Estella," Annie relented.

"You all can call me Cedar, if you want." Estella pulled the vixen into a small hug. When the small vixen pulled away, she found she had been slipped two cookies wrapped in a napkin. The masked rabbit shot her a knowing look as the young vixen hid an impish smile.

"Well, Cedar, these are my other sisters, Mia," Bailey indicated the pregnant vixen, "and Dora." She nodded toward the remaining sister.

"Great to put a face with a name." Mia smiled.

"We've heard so much about you," Dora said.

"I swear only half of it is true," Estella said. They all chuckled as they exchanged pleasantries.

"I'm sorry if I'm a bit low energy," Mia stated. "My kits are taking their sweet time coming out and meeting everyone." She indicated her extremely pregnant belly.

"Trust me. It's better that they wait. They can sleep through the winter and can emerge energized in the spring. Plus, you never want to spend the summer pregnant," Estella said.

Dora gave her a questioning look. "Big family?"

"Smaller now," Estella replied. The vixen sisters gave a small nod of understanding.

"And, of course, the newest addition," Bailey held Ginger in her arms. "At least until Mia's kits decide to join us. This is my pride and joy," Bailey boasted. "Ginger." She handed her daughter to the masked rabbit.

"You're such a big girl!" Estella praised her.

"She's growing alright!" Bailey exclaimed. "She just recently started eating solid food, but she's not completely weaned yet."

"That just means she'll be nice and cuddly for the winter." Estella hiked the youngling up once to get a better grip.

"Absolutely," Bailey agreed. "When spring returns, she will be ready to forage."

Estella held the vixen with one arm as she produced a cherry.

"May I?" she asked Bailey. Bailey nodded.

Estella took the cherry under her mask, split it, removed the seed, and gave half to the young vixen in her arms. Ginger took it, smiling widely, before nuzzling deeper into the masked rabbit's embrace.

As the only tods of the group watching the interaction, Castor shot his brother a knowing smirk, and Ridley returned it with a scowl.

"She never takes to strangers like that," Bailey commented knowingly.

"Guess I'm just lucky," Estella stated.

"Attention, everyone!" a voice called out.

"That's our cue." Bailey took back her daughter from the masked rabbit's arms. Upon being lifted, the foxling objected and reached her tiny paws back toward Estella.

"Looks like you'll have to sit with us," Bailey concluded. The group of vixens led Castor and the odd pair towards the Elder's stage.

"You should know," Bailey addressed Ridley as they walked near the back of their lot, "I pride myself in my daughter being an excellent judge of character."

"I don't know. She spends a lot of time with my brother," Ridley retorted.

"He's sweet with us," Bailey replied.

"I'll bet," Ridley commented dryly.

Bailey turned to him in earnest, a serious expression cloaking her features. "I know you find it hard to believe, but your brother treats us well."

"He had better."

Sensing that both parties had said what they wanted to say, Bailey dropped the topic and rejoined her sisters. Ridley, whether consciously or unconsciously, placed himself between Estella and Castor.

As the group settled, the odd pair, together with Castor, his mate, and daughter, the Elder stood and addressed the crowd. "This story might hit close to home."

Chapter 20

To Live is to Learn

There once lived a family of foxes, a mother, father, and three kits—two teenage boys and a girl of about seven. One day, the father went hunting, and the girl asked if she could pick strawberries. Her mother said she could, but only if her brothers went with her. They agreed.

Before they left, the mother gave the siblings specific instructions. "Remember to stay on the path. Don't go where you've never gone before and be back before the sun starts to set. Most importantly, don't go off on your own."

"Yes, Mother," the foxlings said in unison.

They grabbed their baskets and started on the beaten path. The youngest started skipping and singing, "The sky and river are my friends. They carry air and water to me." The eldest sang along softly, while the middle child went out of his way not to take part. Once they arrived, they all began picking the strawberries. The oldest boy focused on the biggest ones, the youngest focused on the ripest, and the middle foxling picked indiscriminately.

The youngest looked over at the oldest as he picked one with a green base. "Shouldn't we wait until it's all the way red? Mother says only pick the ones that are ripe."

"I've picked with Father before, and we sometimes leave the big ones to ripen. Before we come back, they fall to the ground and shrivel.

They're not worth eating then."

"I guess," the youngest said, not fully convinced.

The eldest then took the opportunity to examine their haul. His vessel was almost full of large strawberries, ranging from good to almost perfect. The youngest's basket was about three-quarters full of the best-looking ones, and the middle sibling's container was only half full with several that weren't close to being ripe.

"You're picking too early. These are going to be way too sour," the big brother scolded his brother.

"They taste the same once they're in a pie." The middle fox defended himself.

"Mother's good, but she can't make something out of nothing."

"You want me to put them back?" the middle fox shot back sarcastically.

"Just be more careful picking." The brother returned to picking. After a few more minutes, the bushes yielded no more ripe strawberries.

"We should head back," the sister declared.

"In a bit," the eldest said, plucking the best-looking strawberry from his own basket and brushing it off with his fur.

"We're going to check something out. Why don't you head back? That way. Mother will have a pie ready by the time we return." The older brother handed her his basket and presented a strawberry to her.

She took the basket and berry. "Alright, but remember to stay on the path." The young foxling took off running, careful not to spill her cargo.

"Where are we going?" the middle fox asked his brother.

"There's a blackberry or raspberry bush, possibly both, down the path a way." They started down the path.

"How do you know?" the middle fox asked.

"Dad told me about it." He sampled a strawberry he had saved for himself.

"Why didn't we bring sister?" the middle fox asked.

"One, the berries might not be ripe yet," the eldest replied. "Second, the bushes are typically covered in thorns, and sister's not ready for those." The foxes continued down the path.

"Wait, shouldn't we have given sister my basket?" the middle fox asked.

"We still need something to carry the berries in." The eldest fox ruffled the top of his brother's head.

After a while, the foxes came to a tree. The older brother looked at it and turned off the path.

"Shouldn't we stay on the path?" the middle fox asked.

"See the indentations." The eldest pointed to the line of tramped grass. "That means Father or some other fox went down the path already." He followed the makeshift path with the middle fox tailing behind. He couldn't see the path as well as his brother but figured he could find the main path when heading back. The trees began to cover the sun, and shadows stretched as the pair made their way through the woods. The eldest fox stopped abruptly.

"We're being watched," he said. "Let's go back." He turned and started back.

"We can't go back now. We haven't seen the berry bushes yet."

"We need to head back."

"Why? Because you think there's some dark monster in these woods?" the middle sibling mocked.

"It's not worth it," the eldest fox said.

"I'm not leaving without those berries." The middle sibling stubbornly refused to move.

"Fine," the eldest said, turning to his brother. "Noon was hours ago, so the sun is currently in the west. We headed north from the path, so the path is now to the south of us. Our den is due east up the mountain hill." The eldest turned and headed back towards the path.

The middle fox scoffed and trekked deeper into the forest. "I'll fill my basket with berries, and then Mother will make a wild berry pie that will blow them all away." He moved a branch aside and walked face-first into a spiderweb. Spinning around, he tried to clear the translucent substance from his eyes and frantically brushed the webbing from his fur. Even after he felt that he had gotten the spiderweb off, he could feel something crawling across his skin.

He stooped down and tried to pick up the strawberries that had fallen out when he had dropped his basket. He knew he hadn't gotten all of them, but when he arose, he found bigger problems. *I don't know where I am.* He looked for the sun, but it was obscured by trees. *No problem, just find a clearing and find the sun.* After wandering more, he found a clearing and saw the sun. *Great, so let's think. It's late afternoon and the sun goes up in the west... wait no, constellations travel east to west so....* He was confusing himself. That's when he heard rustling. The fox turned toward it.

"Brother!" he called. "Sister?"

No response. If something rustled and didn't answer, he didn't want to find out what it was. The fox picked a direction perpendicular to the sun and sprinted away. After he had run a good distance, he stopped to catch his breath. As he huffed and puffed, he looked around. He didn't recognize anything, and the woods had grown even darker. It was close to, if not already, sunset. The fox was worried. The woods were unkind at night. He wandered further. Finally, he saw the bushes his brother had mentioned. The berries were dark purple and light red, blackberries and raspberries. He hurriedly picked them, only to cut himself. He recoiled. The top of his paw bled freely. He licked the blood off and grabbed a berry from his basket. He popped the berry into his mouth. His brims flared up as his mouth puckered. They were the worst berries he had ever tasted. They were too tart to eat!

He then felt something grab the back of his scruff. "You're dead!" an assailant yelled. The fox's heart leapt into his throat. He turned his tear-filled eyes towards his attacker. His heart sank.

"Father!" He gasped as his father grabbed him and his basket. He half-dragged, half-carried his son out of the forest. Only after they got back to the path and walked a way down it did the father hand his son back his basket and let him walk on his own. When they were nearly home, they saw the eldest sibling walking towards them.

"Mother sent me to..." He was cut short by a glare from their father. The trio remained silent as they made their way back to the den. When they arrived, the father gave his satchel full of herbs and meat to his wife and ordered his kits to sit at the dinner table.

"I was watching you three," he began, "and I have some notes."

He turned to his youngest and only daughter. "You followed your mother's and my instructions to the letter. Well done." The young vixen smiled but calmed herself to listen to what else he had to say.

He turned to his eldest son, "You went off the path and led your brother into the woods. That wasn't very smart." The eldest looked down in shame. "However, you kept yourself grounded, rational, and were able to tell when someone was following you." The father tilted his son's face up to look at him. "I won't always be around, and there will be things you will have to discover on your own. You showed good instincts today." The father gave a stern nod of approval. The eldest fox nodded back in understanding.

The father then turned to his second son. "Where to start with you?" The foxling lowered his red face. "Would you like to own up to your own mistakes?"

The foxling lifted his head, "If brother is the one who led us into the forest, why am I the one being scolded?"

"I'll take that as a no," the father sighed. "For starters, I've looked over the baskets of fruit you and your siblings picked. They seem to follow your mother's and my instructions, but you seem incapable or unwilling."

"I guess I could pick berries better."

"You then walked into an unfamiliar forest and continued down an unknown path to find something you'd never seen before, ignoring warnings as you did so." the father snarled.

"I was following my brother, who then left me there. Why isn't he in trouble?" the foxling defended himself.

"Your brother was able to sense danger when it came up and displayed instincts and knowledge from lessons your mother and I have taught him. He then left you to make your own mistakes once you refused to listen." The father slammed his paws on the table. The foxling resigned himself to his fate.

"You didn't notice the danger until it was far too close to you. Your applications of the lessons we taught you left you more confused. I wonder if you didn't understand, or you didn't care. You then left yourself exposed." He walked around and lifted his son's head so that he faced him. "If I were anything else, you would be dead. Do you understand?"

The middle fox forced himself to look at his father, "Yes," he replied.

"Yes, sir," his father corrected him.

"Yes, sir."

The father looked at his foxlings. "I'm only telling you this because I love you all. Do you understand?"

"Yes," they replied. The youngest frantically nodded, the eldest gave a single solemn nod, and the middle foxling kept his head still.

"Set the table," the father said, and the foxlings obeyed.

The mother was prepared to serve the meal when her husband stopped her. "I'm taking our boys hunting tomorrow." He turned to the middle child. "Obey my orders at all times. If you go off on your own tomorrow, I won't be able to save you."

"Yes, sir."

The father turned to the eldest foxling, "You've earned the right to ask questions. I trust they will be studious."

"Yes, sir."

The father turned to the youngest foxling, "You will stay with your mother to see what types of tricks she can teach you."

"I can think of a few." His wife smiled slyly and winked.

"Yes, sir," the youngest said and turned toward her mother, "and yes, ma'am."

"Good." The mother fox served dinner to her family. They all joined paws and said grace.

The father fox turned to the middle son. "Now have you learned your lesson?"

Chapter 21

Mountain Stomp

"Tell me, my fine fellow foxes," the Elder addressed the audience directly, "have you learned your lesson?"

A few solemn nods were seen through the crowd. Scolding looks from parents made their way to select kits and a few indiscriminately. The kits either wilted or scoffed.

"What we must remember, however, is that it truly takes a village to raise a kit, like a congregation such as we have," the Elder stated. "So, it is time for us to come together once more — on the dance floor!"

The vulpine took the invitation and migrated to the dance floor. The odd pair was swept up with the vixen sisters. Once the congregation arrived in full, the Elder stood by the unlit fire across from the fire that had been lit two nights earlier.

"Now," the Elder addressed the audience. "It is the nature of God's creatures to try and prove themselves the best, both within their own ranks and among all others. Hopefully, we got that out of our systems the third night," he said. The male from the winning pair gave a meager wallop at his mention, clearly still tired despite skipping the previous night.

"But tonight is the time we remember that it takes numbers, cooperation, a community, and a tribe to move mountains or rise when we have fallen. More importantly, only together can we ensure the continuation of our values and traditions."

Nods and shouts of agreement flowed through the crowd like a wave.

"Now we must divide the tasks between those who shall cheer and those who shall carry. The carriers will stay where they are, and those cheering will move to either side." Following the announcement, the odd pair helped Dora carry the pregnant Mia off to the cheering side.

"You and Cedar don't have to sit out on our account," Mia told the odd pair once they settled with the group.

"It's alright. We weren't planning to dance anyway," Ridley replied.

"Come on, Riddles, a pretty vixen wants to dance with you," Castor interjected, carrying Ginger in both arms. "If anything can get my kit brother dancing, I'd figure it would be that."

The masked rabbit ghosted a glance towards her fox, and he responded with the slightest of head shakes. "We're not much for dancing." Ridley cut off all questions to the contrary.

"Now those left to carry, split yourselves into two groups. I suggest taking a partner from the other group." The Elder declared. From the remaining group, several vulpine stepped forward while others stepped back. Some clasp paws as they walked together into the front group, and others pointed to the partners in the other group.

"May the first-round step forward," the Elder called. Those in the first group of carriers stepped onto the dance floor.

The Elder lifted the torch and turned towards the setting sun. "It is our duty to carry light into the darkness, and tonight, together as a congregation, we will say goodbye to the sun and be the light of the world until it comes back up. Carriers keep dancing, backups be ready to switch out, and cheerers keep them energized!" The last of the sunlight dipped below the horizon. At that point, the Elder tossed the torch into the unlit bonfire. "Begin!" he exclaimed as the blaze ignited.

The dance floor erupted as the first group of carriers began to dance. The music swelled and filled the air. The cheerers clapped and stomped their paws as the carriers moved and danced in every way imaginable.

After a while the Elder yelled, "Switch!" and the first group of carriers traded places with the second, starting the dance with newfound energy.

"Don't feel left out. Everyone join in!" the Elder exclaimed. Several cheerers took this cue to join their fellow vulpine on the dance floor. Others, including the odd pair, held back with their group. Estella glanced over at her fox and noticed that he was humming under his breath and tapping the toes of his paw.

"Switch!" the Elder called. As the groups traded places and the cheerers filtered back in, the masked rabbit grabbed her fox's paw and pulled him along with her.

"Yeah!" Caster cried out to the pair. The vixen sisters whistled and clapped.

The fox caught his breath as his partner led him into the dancing circle. Rather than attempt the elaborate kicks the other couples were performing, the rabbit instead stomped her feet to a beat unheard by the rest of the company. The fox tried to match the rabbit's rhythm but kept stomping too late or too early.

"Move your tail when you raise your leg," Estella instructed him. The fox did as he was instructed, and it worked instantly. The duo was finally stomping in sync with each other, creating their own beat. Once the fox heard the beat the rabbit had started, his tail wagged from the dance and his excitement.

Other dancers saw this display and tried to imitate it. After a few attempts, they were stomping to the new beat. The onlookers picked it up as well, clapping along, transforming the song and display into something extraordinary. Once the song ended, the Elder raised his paw, and the band went silent. All eyes watched as the Elder made his way off the stage and walked straight towards the masked rabbit and her fox. Once he reached the odd couple, he looked down at the rabbit.

"What's your name?" he asked.

"Estella," the masked rabbit answered, "but my friends call me Cedar."

"Estella." The Elder tasted her name on his lips. "That's a beautiful name."

"Thank you." Estella's heart hammered.

"Where did you learn that little dance of yours?" the Elder inquired.

"It's a dance my family does," Estella answered honestly. "It's called Mountain Stomp."

"Mountain Stomp," the Elder rolled the words over his tongue. He then threw back his head and laughed.

"You younglings should pay attention. Nobody has danced like that in years. Our feet were alive, and we couldn't stop if we wanted to." He turned to the masked rabbit, "Like we're trying to make the mountain move!"

He turned back to the crowd, "This little lady rediscovered a lost art! Without even trying!" The Elder turned to the band, "Start it fast and don't stop. And you," he pointed to a red female fox holding a fiddle, "cut loose! I'm going to show these foxlings the Riverside Shuffle."

The face of the red vixen with the fiddle lit up as if she had been waiting her entire life to hear those words. She began to play as if the woods themselves had summoned her to whip the crowd into a dancing frenzy. He stood before the crowd before moving his feet. When he did, his motions seemed simultaneously random and yet practiced. His stomp held power and rhythm that quickly swept through the whole festival. All the foxes there danced and clapped along to the infectious beat, while others tried to copy the Elder's mesmerizing movements. The odd couple kept with the variation they had created. The whole festival danced until the sun peaked over the horizon.

"I'm starting to see why you vulpine dance so much," Estella commented. She and Ridley slowly made their way on tired legs and sore feet to his den. The growing sunlight cast rays and shadows on the beaten path. "It makes hibernation that much easier."

"That and the food," Ridley said. "I feel like I could sleep for a year."

"We'll have to get rested up for tonight," Estella said, "and I could really go for more of that soup."

Ridley chuckled, "If you can stay awake that long."

"For the soup, I'll stay up later than you," she smirked back.

Once they reached the den, Estella opened the door. When she crossed the threshold, she looked back to see Ridley standing at the door watching her.

"What?" she asked.

"Nothing." He hid his smile before crossing the threshold to join her.

Estella stayed awake long enough for tea but fell asleep before the soup was warm. Ridley wrapped her in a blanket and lay on the ground next to her. He was asleep within seconds.

Chapter 22

Budding

The long nap, as Estella put it, was what the odd couple needed to bounce into another night of the festival. After a small bowl of soup, some light self-grooming, and the now customary application of ash, ribbons, and mask, Estella and Ridley were ready for the sixth night of the festival. To be on the safe side, they stopped at what they now considered their clearing to apply the leftover cedar cinders to the base of her neck.

"There isn't going to be another dance contest, is there?" Estella asked.

"There won't, but tonight will include pairing up again." Ridley finished his work. "So, you should stay close to me."

"If you wanted to dance with me, you could have just asked."

"That's not…." Ridley shook his head. "Tell you what. Once the music starts, we dance with whoever is next to us."

"Sounds like a plan." Estella put on her mask. The odd pair continued towards the festival, secretly exchanging glances.

As they crossed the threshold, the masked rabbit took stock of the now familiar clearing. There was the familiar grouping of families along with couples, young and old. The addition came in the form of packs of vulpine of the same sex grouping together.

"I thought you said tonight was about pairing up." the rabbit said.

"It is," Ridley replied, "but foxes mate for life, and when foxes get desperate, they stop getting picky. The packs are to protect tods and vixens alike from their desperate parallels and, frankly, from themselves."

Cedar continued scanning the crowd. She noticed the lone foxes looking between groups, distressed looks creeping into their features.

She noticed Jazz among the foxes, standing off to the side by herself. When Jazz noticed her, the vixen turned up her face in a scowl. Cedar turned away and disregarded her entirely.

"Attention, everyone!" the Elder called. Vulpine of all kinds turned towards the center stage. "I know you are all desperate to sample the sweeter side of life, but I find it paramount to say, 'While it pays to be picky, perfect is the enemy of good.'"

A select few mature vulpine in the congregation nodded while other immature ones scoffed.

"Let us pray." The Elder blessed the meal, and the congregation of vulpine broke towards the banquet table. The odd pair moved to their usual opposite sides. For whatever reason, there was more pushing and shoving than there had been the previous nights. When Ceder looked up, she could no longer find her fox.

"Oof," she hissed as she was bumped once more.

"Sorry," the black and red tod said. The tod then did a double take.

"I know you."

Cedar looked up at the fox. She tried to remember his face but couldn't place him. "I don't think…"

"You're the masked mountain vixen," the tod interrupted. Cedar was annoyed, a little flattered, and slightly perplexed.

"I prefer Cedar," she replied.

"Right, Cedar. Hey, if you're not too tired from last night, I'd love to dance with you."

Fear boiled in the pit of her stomach. "I'm actually with someone," she stammered.

The red and black fox faked a glance around the area. "I don't see him around." He shot her a grin that was supposed to be charming but came off as cocky. "That means you're available to dance."

They had reached the end of the table, and Cedar's voice caught in her throat. She tried to swallow the lump but found her throat too dry.

"She can't!" A gray tod pushed his way forward. Before Cedar could feel relieved, the gray fox continued, "She already promised to dance with me!"

The gray fox was as much a stranger to her as the red and black one, and neither seemed inclined to take no for an answer.

"You're Cedar, right?" A vixen appeared in front of the masked rabbit. Her slick black fur gave her the appearance of a mink.

"Yyyees," the masked rabbit stammered.

"You should come with me," the mink-like vixen said. Cedar took a half step toward her before the vixen remarked, "I have a brother who would love to meet you."

"'Exc..cu..cuse me, Cceedar," a red fox, smaller than the other tods and the vixen, stammered in excitement. Would you like to dance?" he inhaled, "With me?"

Never had the masked rabbit felt more frightened. She was cornered by four foxes. Every instinct, conscious, unconscious, and otherworldly, screamed at her to run. Instead, she froze. Her heart hammered in her throat, and her head buzzed like a kicked beehive.

"Estella!" The masked rabbit saw a vixen in a red dress and gold sash approach.

"Xin," Estella sighed. "What's keeping you?"

"I was just asking this little vixen if she'd like to dance," the red and black fox stated.

"She said she'd dance with me," the grey fox remarked.

"I don't remember her saying yes," the black vixen interjected.

"I also asked!" the red tod raised his paw to nobody in particular.

Xin subtly placed herself between Estella and the other vulpine. "I can see you all want the company of this young lady."

"None more than me!" the paltering gray fox announced.

"We'll do this fairly." Xin held up a grape. "Whoever catches the grape in his mouth, gets the pleasure of her company."

"I'm game!" the boisterous red and black tod declared.

"Let's do it," said the insistent black vixen. The group of vulpine surrounded Xin, eyes on the grape held between the vixen's claws.

"Grapes and quail!" Xin called, tossing the grape into the air.

"Grapes and quail!" the makeshift pack responded. Estella focused her sight on the flying grape, careful not to lose it in the night sky. Before the masked rabbit could question Xin's actions, the vixen noiselessly whisked her away so the other vulpine didn't notice they were gone.

"Now, would I be correct in assuming that you wish to be with Ridley?" Xin asked.

"Yes," she answered, "and thank you."

"Don't mention it," Xin replied. "As you can tell, foxes of all kinds tend to get desperate on the sixth night."

"That's one way of putting it." Estella paused for a moment.

"There's no king and queen of the festival is there?"

"Not while I've been coming," Xin responded. "The closest we get is the dance champion from the third night, but outside of their names carved on the stones, they don't get any other special recognition."

"Good." Estella breathed. "I was starting to think they were about to elect me festival queen or something."

Xin gave her a quizzical look. "You don't like being the center of attention, do you?"

"When it comes to company, I prefer quality to quantity."

"I'll take that as a compliment." Xin smiled.

"It was meant as one."

Finally, Estella and Xin found Ridley. When she saw him, Estella rushed forward and hugged the tod. He was startled for the briefest moments before wrapping his arms around the cinder-stained beauty.

"I lost you," Ridley stated.

"I got mobbed by a skulk of foxes. They either wanted to dance with me or set me up with one of their family members."

Ridley looked at her sternly, "You didn't agree to anything, did you?"

"No, I don't think so," Estella stammered.

"You got to be careful, especially when it comes to the festival. You might volunteer for something without even knowing it," Ridley chided.

"Does that happen a lot?"

"More often than you think. I offered to help with the banquet table setup three years ago, and they worked my paw pads to stumps, hauling trays," Ridley grumbled.

Xin gave him a jaded look. "You don't know work until you've toiled under my mother and *really* worked the banquet table."

Ridley gave her a puzzled look, "I've never seen you work the trays."

"Because we make the food! My mom and I handle over half the jams and jellies that go into all the desserts!" Xin exclaimed. "Do you know how hard it is to seal and reopen jars?"

"Attention, everyone!" a voice called. The little group and all the others took that as the sign to head for the stage.

"We'll have to meet Baset and my treasures at the stage," Xin stated without turning her back to the others.

Ridley reached down within earshot of Estella. "Let's hope nobody calls you up to sing on stage."

Under her mask, Estella wore a puzzled look. She didn't know if her fox was serious.

Once the vulpine had settled, the Elder addressed them. "This is to remind us of the things that happened only yesterday."

Chapter 23

Riverside Kindling

There once were four foxes of different households, but a pack nonetheless. The pack consisted of two males and two females. The males were both red foxes, one with a slender athletic build and the other portlier. The females were light gray and black, respectively.

It was no secret to all who happened to glance at them that the athletic male and the grey female were deeply in love. Only the black fox failed to know that the larger male harbored the deepest affection for her. Everyone knew, except the larger male, that she returned the affection.

One day in late summer, the four foxes made their way to the local riverbanks for a swim. They took turns on the rope swing tied to the tree. The foxes, young and in love, were more focused on who could make the biggest splash or strike the silliest pose before hitting the water.

The athletic fox was the first to notice a ripple in the water. He was halfway through his swing and planned to point back at the others as his back hit the water. His instincts kicked in. Instead of a pose, he dismounted from the rope as it reached its peak, angled his body headfirst, and made a perfect dive into the water. Seconds later, he appeared with a fish between his jaws. The others walloped and hollered upon seeing the feat. The athletic fox swam back to the shore and basked in their adoration. He then pulled the gray fox aside.

"Share the fish with me," he said through gritted teeth. They ate his catch together before meeting in the middle for a kiss.

The larger fox looked at the exchange with envy. "My turn," he called to his pack, "and I'll catch a bigger one!"

"I couldn't do that again if I tried," the other red fox told him.

"Well, now I'm trying," the larger red fox stated. He grabbed the rope and swung out. Trying to replicate the dive, he overshot and landed on his back.

"I think that won the biggest splash award!" the athletic fox called to him. The others laughed. If it were possible, the larger fox would have turned redder because they were laughing at him.

He tried again, but he belly flopped. He tried a third time but landed feet first. He tried once again, but he fell before the rope reached the end of its arc.

He kept trying, even when the others said he didn't have to. He didn't stop when they left the rope swing to swim in their chosen space. Even when they stopped swimming altogether and sat on the riverbank. When the other red fox and gray fox left together, the portly fox refused to quit.

After his latest failed attempt, the larger red fox looked and saw that the black fox was the only one left. He was grateful his extreme blushing would not show through his red fur. He fell to his knees to suppress a sob. The black fox walked over to him.

"I scared away all the fish, didn't I?" he asked, not looking up.

"I think we all scared away the fish when we first got here. Red friend just got extremely lucky," the black fox replied.

"I figured that out by about my third try, but I...," his voice caught in his throat.

"You didn't have to catch another fish. We weren't laughing at you." The black fox sat next to him and began to stroke his fur.

"But I needed to catch one, so then I could share it with you."

She blinked back. "You were trying to catch a fish — for me?"

The red fox froze. "We should probably head back."

"Yeah, we should," the black fox agreed. They began to walk back when the red fox turned to the black vixen beside him.

"Can I tell you something?" he asked.

"Sure."

The red fox waited a minute. "I'll tell you tomorrow."

"Alright, if I have to wait, I will."

Chapter 24

Blooming

The Elder finished, and the crowd erupted in applause. "Now I won't keep y'all any longer. "Go find that someone special and show them what they mean to you. That's an order."

As if on command, the vulpine moved towards the dance floor. Some groups stayed in their packs as more zealous individuals tried to ambush unwary dance partners.

"Hey Estella, neither of us were able to get food from the table and I'm starving. Can you come with me?" Xin asked.

"Sure."

"I'll come with you, too," Ridley said.

"No need," Xin replied. "We'll keep each other honest and out of trouble. You take the kits to the band and start dancing."

The two vixens headed towards the banquet table while the tods led the kits to where the music swelled.

"Were you two planning on dancing tonight? I know you're not shy," Baset questioned his golden-eyed brother.

"We were just going to take tonight as it comes," Ridley replied.

"Wise way to live."

When the brothers arrived, the music was light and energetic. There were a few couples scattered among them, but most vulpine danced alone, hoping to catch the eye of an attractive mate.

"You and Delia should do your dance," Baset addressed his son. Felix moaned, and Delia rolled her eyes at the suggestion.

"Do we have to?" they asked.

"Well, if you two don't want to dance with each other, I suppose I could set both of you up with some nice young kits. How does that sound?" Baset mused.

The twin foxlings looked at each other as they had done a thousand times and gave a mutual nod of understanding. Wordlessly, they took each other's paw and strode onto the dance floor. The duo danced in a sequence only they knew. Each action was the perfect mirror of their twin. They flowed as their movements rose and flew, sped up and slowed down. They were like twin torches, the flare and flicker of flames. The vulpine patrons took notice and began to watch, clapping and cheering along with the music. The dance ended with a fantastical twirl and a mutual bow. The crowd clapped and cheered in jubilation.

"Enjoy it," Baset said to the fox next to him. "It'll probably be the last time they do that."

"Why?" Ridley questioned. "They were good, and it looked like they had fun."

"Yeah, but they're getting older," Baset explained. "By this time next year, they won't want to do that. They probably won't even want to spend time with us. They'll just be running off to try and prove themselves. It's the one thing about parenting people never tell you, and one thing from childhood you forget," Baset turned to Ridley.

"Remember the riverbanks?"

"The best times."

"You always were trying to run after us larger foxes. You thought being the eldest meant you belonged with the bigger foxes. You were always thinking the best of life was on the other side of whatever you couldn't see."

"Were we ever that young?" Ridley shook his head at the memories.

"You want to know a secret, Mr. Riverbank Ridley?"

"I'm game."

"Xin can't sing," Baset stated.

Ridley raised his eyebrows. "She can't? But her voice is...,"

"Her voice is smooth, but she struggles with tone and pitch." He looked over at his children as they basked in the praise of the vulpine crowd.

"But the kids insist that she sing to them every night before bed." Baset smiled. "The onlooker might not think it's anything special, but to me, it's the most beautiful singing in the world."

"Secret to life?"

"One of many." Baset sighed. "Or maybe there is no secret. You'll have to figure that out for yourself, Kit." Baset winked at his brother before disappearing into the crowded sea of vulpine to rejoin his wife.

Ridley looked back and saw that after the twins had finished their dance routine, they took one final bow before blending in with the crowd of dancers. He scanned the crowd. Like a vision, his masked rabbit stepped into the clearing. He rushed over to her.

"Hey, I was coming back with Xin and she disapp...," Estella started.

"May I have this dance?" Ridley offered her his paw.

Estella's eyes lit up. "I'd love to." She missed a breath as Ridley took her paw and whisked her onto the dance floor.

It was safe to say Ridley had never seen his rabbit like this. Gone was the nervous thumping and ticks that had accompanied the masked beauty those first few nights. Now, she not only moved lightly across the ground, but she had added a little sway to her step. Whether intentional or not, her strut was driving the fox crazy.

"Still think you're going to be struck by lightning?" Ridley playfully sniffed her cheek.

"Please, my good sir," Estella teased back, "I'm more likely to fall in love at first sight, and that simply can't happen."

"So, you still take trees over lightning?"

"Of course, trees can withstand lightning strikes with little more than a mark of peeled bark. The tree lives while the lightning ceases to exist," Estella waxed philosophically.

"Unless the tree catches fire," Ridley retorted, playing the game she had started.

"Only if it hits the sap."

Ridley looked puzzled, "The sap is flammable?"

"No. The lightning superheats the sap, and that's what causes the fire."

"How do you know that?"

"One of my uncles got struck by lightning. He kept talking about ground, trees, and cold, smooth rocks after that. Nobody understood it."

"Sorry, I'm still stuck on uncle struck by lightning!"

Without warning, Estella burst out laughing, a full-on, hunched-over, side-splitting belly laugh. It must've been contagious as Ridley started laughing, too. Minutes passed before the pair could regain their composure.

"I'm sorry." Estella wiped tears from her eyes. "When you're a rabbit, you end up meeting only half your relatives, and the other half you will swear are made up."

Ridley chuckled harder. "I don't know, but the crazy rabbit struck by lightning sounds pretty credible."

"What about the cousin who jumped so high he landed in a tree branch and couldn't get himself down?" Estella asked.

"We all have cousins like that," Ridley stated.

"What about the part where the uncle covers himself in mud and tries to cut the tree down with his teeth like a beaver?"

"No." Ridley shook his head.

"But the tree had ivy growing on it. His teeth itched for weeks!" Estella exclaimed.

Ridley snorted a laugh. "You're making this up."

"These were the stories I was told. I'm just now realizing how absurd they are."

"I don't know," Ridley mused. "They seem just the kind of kin to be related to a rabbit who dresses in cedar cinders and goes to the Fox Fire Festival."

Estella huffed, this time in good spirits. "Maybe we'll have to find the other half of my family I've never met. I can introduce them to you."

"I don't see that going well," Ridley said.

"I may have to tie your mouth shut, but I think it would work."

"I can play nice," Ridley said, "so long as none of them mess with my tail."

"It's settled then. I'll be the crazy aunt who fell for a fox, and you can be the cool uncle who eats the kits who bully our nieces and nephews." Estella wrapped her arms around her tall fox's shoulders.

Ridley questioned, "You fell for a fox, did you?"

Estella raised her mask to look into the eyes of her fox. She fluttered her eyelashes and drew a finger down his brims and jawline. "You grew on me." She turned and walked further down the path. Ridley stood in silence for several moments. The ghost of a glance that Estella shot behind her released him from his stupor.

"Spend the winter with me!" Ridley called out.

Estella turned back, "What?"

"You heard me. Spend the winter with me," he repeated.

Estella returned to her position, hanging from Ridley's shoulders.

"Convince me."

"I have more than enough food and space and ...." He paused. "I don't want to wait until the end of winter to see you again."

Estella shrugged her shoulders, "I don't know. I'll have to weigh my options."

Now, he knew she was being coy. She had no other options, and they both knew it. Still, she wanted him to convince her. How a rabbit had outfoxed him, he would spend the next several years trying to figure out.

"I swear I can make the soup correctly this time," Ridley stated.

"Good to know."

"I won't hog the bed or the covers."

"I'm small, not much of a problem."

Ridley thought for a moment. "I want you to be the first thing I see when I wake up in the spring."

Estella rolled her eyes. "Are you going to kiss me or not?"

Ridley responded with a half-caressing kiss on her crown.

Estella shook her head. "Nope." She repeated her jawline trace.

Their muzzles met in a tender kiss. Ridley smiled, exposing his brims.

Estella kissed them before pulling back. Both took a moment.

"You have a nice smile," Estella told her fox.

Ridley shrugged his shoulders. "I wouldn't know."

"Well, I don't know about you, Mr. Riverbank Ridley." Estella began walking toward the den. "But, I'm going to find a fox to cuddle up with tonight."

Ridley followed behind her. He couldn't stop grinning from ear to ear.

Chapter 25

Last Night of the Masked Rabbit

Ridley poured water over the final cedar wood fire. He looked over at Estella. While she had gotten proficient at applying her disguise, they went through the routine of preparation. As Ridley applied the ashes to the crown of her head, Estella wore a warm smile of intimacy. Ridley, however, looked more downcast than he had in days. As he caressed her neck applying the cinders, she took hold of his paw and let it open onto her cheek. She leaned into his paw and gazed into his eyes with her sapphires.

"Let's not go tonight," Ridley answered Estella's unspoken question.

"We're already here, and I'm already dressed," Estella answered.

"Still, I have a bad feeling about tonight. Let's call it an early night."

"We will." Estella nodded. "But I want to see the final fire lit and say hi to your mom. Then we can leave right after tonight's story."

He pressed his forehead into her crown. They deeply inhaled each other's scents.

"Promise me you'll be careful?"

Estella nodded. "I promise."

They walked the short distance to the clearing. The odd pair grasped each other's paws as they crossed the threshold of the Fire Festival for the final time. The guests were fairly dispersed into various groups. Tired foxes regretted coming, while young ones were energetic and trying to make the most of the final night. Couples, old and new, cuddled around the various bonfires, while tods and vixens alike tried to find someone to pair up with before the first frost set in. Kits of all kinds played with an energy that hadn't diminished in all the late nights and dancing marathons. Parents, elders, and family friends watched contently by the glow of the fires.

Some dressed in their best attire while others were in more casual garb. What stood out, however, was the abundance of male and female foxes wearing wooden masks and with their tails wrapped around their waists.

"Looks like you're quite the trendsetter," Ridley observed.

"Unless people start marking themselves with ashes, I wouldn't worry about it," Estella answered.

"Like anybody but you could pull it off," Ridley flirted. This earned him an eyeroll, but he knew she had a coy smile under her mask.

"River, my boy, and the beautiful Cedar wood flower! How are you, youngins?" a voice called. The pair turned to see Clark walking towards them, carrying a plate of roast quail covered in grape jelly and an orange sauce the rabbit couldn't identify. Behind him, Lana shambled up, biting into a juicy overripe peach and carrying a tray of square pastries.

The older fox held out his paw. As Ridley reached out, Clark stuck his paw under Ridley's.

"Snail!" Clark exclaimed. "You always fall for that, and I love you for it."

"Oh, stop it." Lana walked to his side and lightly slapped at his stomach.

"Are we late? We didn't hear the go-ahead." Estella indicated the trays of food.

"This might be our last festival, so we're enjoying it while we can," Clark stated.

"No, it isn't! I'm going to see you both next year," Ridley assured them.

"Well, if you say so, we might just have to," Lana answered.

"Still, I don't have much dancing left in me, so we'll leave after the Elder's story and get back to the den before the frost sets in," Clark said.

"We're leaving after the Elder's story, too," Estella replied.

Clark leered at Ridley. "Getting cozy for the winter, are we?"

"Oh, stop it." Lana grabbed Clark's shoulder. She gave a subtle sniff. "Here comes trouble."

"Hey!" Castor called, jogging up to the group.

"Next year, I'm getting a mask," Ridley stated to nobody in particular.

"You know you'd miss me," Castor replied. "Mother's looking for you."

"Tell her I'm not here," Ridley replied.

"Young kit, do not keep her waiting," Lana scorned the younger tod.

"Fine." Ridley relented.

"And she wants Cedar to come to." Castor turned to the masked rabbit. "Or was it Stella?"

"Estella," she clarified.

"Right," Castor nodded.

"Have you been staying out of trouble?" Lana asked Castor.

"Bailey and Ginger are keeping me honest. They're all waiting for us."

"Good," Lana said. "I'd hate to have to wallop you again."

"You never walloped me a first time," Castor retorted.

"You want there to be a first time?" she snarled.

Castor immediately stiffened, "No, ma'am!"

"Good boy." Lana nodded.

Castor turned back to Ridley. "Come on. I've got to get you all back before old man Baset gets his claws into you."

"What about me?" Clark asked.

Castor turned to him. "You, young lad, better respect this young lady," he gestured toward Lana, "and treat her right."

"I'll try." Clark pulled his wife closer to him. Lana rolled her eyes and snickered.

The odd pair nodded goodbye and followed Castor.

Castor led Ridley and Estella to the matron vixen, surrounded by Seren, Bailey, holding Ginger, and Baset, whom she was currently grilling.

"Don't worry I'll find him." Baset turned toward the odd pair. Upon laying eyes on Ridley, he exclaimed, "And here he is! I told you I'd find him."

"My Ridley finally returns to us." Celeste opened her arms.

"Hi, Mom." Ridley wrapped his arms around his welcoming mother.

"Young kit, what have I told you about hiding from your mother?" Baset joked.

"Hide by the crafts table. She'll never look there," Ridley replied.

The vixens shot Baset a side eye.

"I never — said that," Baset stammered. "Well, Ridley is found, and my work here is done. I'm going to see my wife." Baset started off.

"Your family's the other way," Celeste said, not looking toward him.

"I knew that." Baset turned around.

"So, what did you need me for?" Ridley asked his mother.

"I need both of you." Celeste indicated her oldest and the masked rabbit.

"Why?" Estella asked.

Celeste's stern expression turned downcast. "This may be the last time I see you all."

She then pulled Ridley into another hug, licked the base of his ears, and rubbed the bottom of her chin on top of his head. She then made her way to Castor and did the same. All three siblings exchanged knowing and annoyed looks.

"Mother, we will see you in the spring," Seren said as their mother made her way to her.

"I know," Celeste said, starting to mark her daughter. "But without your father...." She stopped talking but continued her important work. The siblings' faces fell. "I miss him." Celeste broke into tears. Seren wrapped her arms around her mother. Ridley and Castor placed their paws on her shoulders.

"We all do," Seren said for everybody.

Celeste let herself be comforted, and then she straightened and regained her composure. "I will miss my Samson every day, but I have my old kits." She looked toward Bailey and Estella. "And my new kits." She reached out to Ginger. "And my new grandkits."

Bailey surrendered Ginger to her grandmother as she began to mark the young foxling. The newborn squirmed, not understanding or welcoming the newfound attention. Once Ginger was marked,

Celeste handed her to Seren as she began to mark Bailey, no stranger to this behavior, but not familiar enough to hide her discomfort.

Upon recognizing Estella, Ginger reached her tiny paws towards her. "Looks like someone misses you." Seren walked over and presented the foxling to Estella. Estella took the newborn, both their eyes shining.

"Did someone miss me?" she playfully asked the newborn. Ginger squealed with delight as she reached out to grab the masked rabbit. Estella cuddled and swooned over the foxling, causing Ginger to giggle.

"Ain't that beautiful?" Castor nudged Ridley. Ridley remained silent but bit back his smile.

Ginger then reached out to grab the side of Estella's head. Her hand flexed, and her claw dug into Estella's flesh.

"Ow!" Estella cried out.

"Sorry. Sorry!" Bailey took back her daughter.

"It's alright. I had younger siblings, and they bit a lot growing up," Estella said reassuringly. Bailey and Seren nodded but hid sorrow behind their eyes.

Celeste came over and wiped the paws of her grandkit. Seren finally spoke up, "Mother, I'm sorry I couldn't find anybody to spend the winter with."

"Don't you worry about it, my darlings." Celeste kissed the crowns of her daughter and granddaughter. "It is no transgression to be picky. You'll be spending the rest of your life with whoever you choose."

She turned to Estella. "I'm just glad my kits have such good taste." She stepped toward the masked rabbit, who unconsciously took half a step back.

"Estella is covered in ashes." Ridley inserted himself between the two. "They cover up burn marks."

"I know," Celeste said. She pulled out a scarlet kerchief and then used it to clean the scratch mark made by her granddaughter. She tied the kerchief around Estella's neck as a makeshift scarf.

Celeste stepped back to admire her handiwork. She was about to withdraw when Estella pulled her into a proper hug. Celeste smiled.

"Welcome to the pack," she whispered.

"Attention, everyone!" a voice called out. "It is time for the final night's story!"

The newly formed pack made their way to the center bonfire pit. The odd pair couldn't stop smiling.

"My fine fellow foxes," the Elder addressed the congregation of vulpine. "It is the last night of our festival. I'm sure everyone has had a wonderful time, and we'll most definitely end tonight with a bang before winter falls upon the land."

Vulpine of all shapes, sizes, and colors nodded in agreement.

"But before that happens, I must ask, who can tell me the purpose of our stories?" The Elder scanned the crowd for an answer.

"They connect us, past and present!" someone shouted.

"To entertain us!" someone else thundered.

"To carry our lessons and culture with us!" yet another called out.

"To move the heavens themselves and bring the horizon back to us!" a vulpine cried out in reverence.

"All good reasons," the Elder said, "but what is that final, most important reason?"

The crowd fell silent until a young vixen stepped forward. "So that we may be redeemed."

The Elder flashed the warmest of smiles. "That is exactly right! Thank you, young kit."

The young vixen bowed before stepping back.

"The stories sustain us, tell us where we've been, where we're going, and what awaits us just over the horizon...."

Chapter 26

The First and Final Fox Fire

On the eighth day of creation, darkness fell over the Garden of Eden. Frightened, the creatures of the garden gathered around the drinking reservoir. In the middle of the blackened pool, the lion stood at attention.

"Creatures of God," the lion addressed the garden's inhabitants. "Eden has fallen. Deceit, malice, and shame have entered the garden and poisoned its grounds. What once produced fruit will now be laden with thorns and thistles, and you will look to each other for sustenance." The creatures of God were frightened.

"How did this happen?" they called amongst themselves.

"Why is this happening?"

"What caused this?

Finally, the great wolf came forward. "How may we fix this?"

The lion once again addressed the creatures of the garden. "There is nothing by your own doing that may cleanse this poisoned ground. Some of you will struggle to forage in this cursed ground known as earth. Some of you will turn on your fellow creature to survive. Some will do both."

A shocked stirring washed over the creatures of God. They wore expressions of terror, disbelief, and shame.

"No!" a voice called out. Large creatures moved out of the way as a lone fox made his way to the front of the group. He addressed the lion.

"You were the one who raised us from the dust! You breathed air into our nostrils! You sang this very world into existence! We have been faithful! We have obeyed! We are not to be discarded!"

Silence descended upon the crowd. Gradually, they all looked to the lion for his response.

Finally, the lion spoke, "You have obeyed. You have learned the lessons Eden has taught you and followed them well. But this I say to you: Your descendants will forget the teachings and be consumed with their own survival until they are once again consumed by the ground itself. It will take generations upon generations, but there may come a day when the lessons are relearned, and the creatures of God will once again know peace. You have, however, shown a great deal of faith. Because of your faith, I offer this. Ascend with me to the heavens, so that we might light the way for those generations. They need only to look up and see our guiding light."

There was a moment before the ram stepped forward, "What must we do?"

The lion nodded. "Come to me and take your place in the night sky."

The ram stepped forward. His hoof touched the water, but he did not sink. As he made his way toward the lion, his body began to shine. Noticing this, the ram began to run toward the lion until he rose from the surface of the pool and began to light the darkening sky.

The other creatures of God followed suit. The wolf led, and the bear and the stag followed, taking their places as leaders and guardians. The smaller lion and lynx walked side by side as they ascended. The giraffe rose higher than the others thought possible. The lizard, crab, and scorpion scurried across the water before rising. The birds of the air flew up, their feathers glistening and falling as stardust as they shed for the final time. Even the creatures of the sea swam out of the pool and into the ever-lightening sky, forever adding their glimmering presence.

Finally, the only creatures left on the ground were the lion and the fox.

"You've yet to join them," the lion stated.

"The night sky is filled," the fox answered. "There is no room left for me."

"You've obeyed until this point. Have you lost your faith?"

"No, I haven't." The fox threw himself on the ground at the lion's feet. "I will not leave this ground until you command me to do so. Please, bless me as you have blessed the others."

"As we speak, there is one who knows me but still asks me my name. He, too, demanded a blessing. For your faith, I will give you the brightest and most mystifying light of them all."

As the lion said this, the fox began to ascend and to radiate light. Reds, blues, purples, and greens mixed as the fox rose into the heavens, leaving a trail of light behind him.

Chapter 27

Divine Revelations

A hush went over the crowd. The masked rabbit had the urge to clap but restrained herself.

The Elder addressed the crowd directly once more, "My fine fellow foxes, I thank you for listening. Thank you for attending the festival and for carrying on our traditions for the generations to come. You have walked in the light of faith, and for your faith, you shall see what awaits us beyond the great horizon."

The crowd's heads rose as the once pitch-black night sky filled with colors. Changing and crashing into each other, waves upon waves of blue, green, purple, and pink flowed through the sky. As they streaked across the heavens, the masked rabbit watched them. The northern lights had transformed into foxes, playing and spreading the light from their tails for all the world to see.

The crowd stood in mesmerized reverence. The Elder addressed the crowd for the final time, "The heavens themselves have shone down on us. We must go and make tonight worthy of those who came before us and remembered by all those who shall come after!"

Upon his address, the vulpine moved into their personal groups. Couples found their secret corners, individuals made their way to the buffet, families wrangled their kits and seniors, dancers headed to the band floor, and others slinked off to cozy up for the approaching winter.

Ridley prepared to slink away with his masked beauty, but Estella pulled him towards the rising music of the band. Once they arrived on the dance floor, he looked at the masked beauty in front of him.

"What are we doing?" Ridley asked.

"Let's have one final dance, and then we'll run away together," Estella whispered to him.

Ridley relented, and the duo began to foxtrot. As the song played, the pair danced closer together. At the band's last burst of music, the fox dipped the masked beauty. The strands holding Estella's mask to her face began to unwind from the sharpness of Ginger's claws earlier that evening. Before either realized it, the mask fell from Estella's face, exposing her to the world. She scrambled to pick it up, but the damage had been done. Every vulpine in or around the dance floor saw Estella for who she was.

"Rabbit!" someone called.

"What's going on?" a fox on the outer rim shouted.

"She's a rabbit!" someone cried out.

Whispers and murmurs swept through the congregation faster than the wind itself.

"She wants our destruction!"

"She has tainted our festival!"

"She is stealing our traditions!"

"She must pay!"

"Seize her!" someone exclaimed.

The vulpine near the masked beauty began to converge. They stopped short by the snap of Ridley's jaws.

"BACK OFF!" he growled, placing himself between Estella and the other vulpine. "SHE'S MINE!" His tail moved of its own accord and wrapped itself loosely around her. "Come near her, and I'll end you! I don't care who! I don't care how many!"

Ridley took every half step, sideways glance, or twitch of a paw as a threat. He snapped his jaws at the vulpine surrounding him and Estella.

Then came the solemn moment. The silence deafened the congregation. The only thing anybody heard was the hammering of his own heart.

"Enough of this!" a voice called out. Then came the thumping of a wooden leg on the hard ground. Lana made her way through the crowd and stood before the couple.

"Enough of this! All of you!" she addressed the crowd. "This young lady came to a party. She danced with us, ate with us, laughed, talked, and made us feel as if we were old friends. She has treated everyone here with the utmost kindness and respect." She brandished her cane. "If anyone has a problem with that, with her, I will wallop them."

"Same goes for me!" Clark said, sauntering up to stand next to his wife. "And y'all know I can wallop every last one of you."

Murmurs rose and fell through the shocked silence of the congregation. Wordlessly, Baset, accompanied by his wife and children, joined the group to stand between Estella and the other vulpine. Seren stepped forward, looked back towards her mother, and then walked over to stand next to Estella.

Castor walked up to face his brother. "Are we doing this?" he asked wearily. Ridley gave him a solemn nod. Castor huffed. "We're doing this." He turned back to the crowd.

"Mess with him or his girl, you mess with me! I'll take anyone and everyone here," he declared.

Bailey made her way through the crowd, cradling Ginger in her arms.

"Bailey don't..." Castor started to warn his wife before she cut him off with a stern look. She handed her daughter to Estella. Ginger snuggled herself into her embrace as if they'd done it a thousand times.

"Look at how my daughter cuddles into her embrace. See how she holds her as if she were her own! Have you all forgotten? Have you all lost yourselves? Where is your honor?"

Bailey then took her daughter back and stood beside Estella. The vixen's sisters made their way through the crowd and joined the group around Estella. Annie stood beside her and held her paw, daring anyone from the other side to defy her.

Soon other foxes made their way to stand with the group protecting the odd couple: the short red fox, the black fox whose fur was combed to look like a minx, the young fiddler vixen, several foxes in aprons, the vixen with the smokey voice and her bandmates, the skinny fox who played the flute, the large drummer, and the fox with a rose pinned to his chest, now brandishing his horn like a club. Even the fox who had walked past them the first night, shouting 'grapes and quail'. Many others whom Estella and Ridley didn't recognize took their place between them and the congregation. Old couples took their place beside Clark and Lana. Teenage tods took their place in guard next to Castor, and adolescent vixens stood beside Bailey and her sisters. Foxlings, barely a year old, stood in front of Estella, arms raised in protection of her.

The remaining congregation stood perplexed at the event unfolding in front of them, unsure of how to react.

Then the Elder raised his paw skyward. A hush fell over the crowd. The odd pair and those who stood by them watched anxiously.

Slowly, the Elder gray fox began speaking, "There are Elders among us who believe that the first Fox Fire was done by a lone fox trying to save a valley and its inhabitants from a harsh winter. Others say it was in Eden itself where a lone fox saved all creatures created by God from being lost, discarded, and forgotten. Both thought little of themselves and worried only of others. Both brought light to those who needed it most—God's creatures great and small. The fox lit the way.

And now we have a guest, who, despite grave danger to her own life and well-being, came to our festival in good faith, so that we may again live as we did in the Land of Eden."

The Elder gave the masked rabbit a warm smile. "You've brought back something we've lost, in more ways than one."

He turned and addressed the crowd once more, "We should follow their example and ensure our light touches all God's creatures, and those who come in good faith shall be welcomed. But as for tonight and all nights that proceed, no harm shall come to our most honored guest."

Those whom the Elder was addressing relented. Those standing with the odd pair let out a collective sigh of relief. Ridley and Estella turned to each other before embracing in joy, disbelief, excitement, absolution, and indescribable peace.

"Now, if I'm not mistaken, I believe there was a festival we were celebrating!" the Elder exclaimed. The crowd on all sides began to cheer when Celeste stepped forward. All eyes turned toward her as ears pricked up in anticipation.

"Ridley," she addressed her son. She turned to the woman formally called Cedar, "Estella." She took a breath. "You are welcome to this festival, our congregation, and my pack." She gave Estella a wistful smile. "So, I don't think you need to wear that mask anymore."

Cheers and clapping rose from the crowd.

Estella gave a nervous smile as she reached up to her masked head. Suddenly, her ear bindings fell away as they had nothing to bind. She felt her ears that were now short and pointed. Her faux tail unwound itself from her waist as a new tail, as pure and white as she was, grew in its place and began wagging. She removed her mask entirely to reveal her snout had grown in length, her teeth sharpened, and her beautiful sapphire eyes could see through the darkness around her. She had truly become a fox.

Everyone stared in stunned silence at the miracle they had just witnessed. The Elder spoke again, "The lights of heaven have shone down on us. What once was old has been made new, and what seemed impossible is now absolute."

Estella, examining her new form, turned to Ridley. "How do I look?" she asked nervously.

Ridley walked over to her, "I don't see a difference. You're still the one I fell for, the one I never thought I'd meet, and the one I'll love forever, if you'll let me." He caressed her cheek, placed his paw on the small of her back, and wrapped his tail around her.

Unconsciously, her new tail wrapped around him as she reached up to caress his face. "Always," she said as she pulled him in for a kiss.

They pressed their foreheads together as the crowd rejoiced, and the light of heaven shone down on the congregation.

The odd couple and their family would return to the festival for years to come, and their story would be told and retold, forever.

Epilogue

*T*he wolf in the tan sweater finished. He closed the book with a contented sigh. "Always warms the heart, this one." He gave the book a loving pat before returning it to the bookshelf.

"That's it?" Riley asked, fearing his time in Saddlebags' library was ending.

"For the first chronicle, yes," Saddles replied. "Many others are waiting to be told." He gestured to the remaining collection in the glass case. His face took on a wistful look.

"That's something the Spirits haven't grasped. They've read hundreds of books, more than most humans will read in their entire lifetimes, and they still haven't figured out the truth — that books end. What humans still haven't figured out yet is that the end of the story is not the true end. It's the beginning of a new one. All we must do is pull it off the shelf, open it, and turn the page," he explained.

"Still hurts to put the book back on the shelf," Riley admitted.

"I find that good books, the truly great ones, keep people coming back to them," Saddlebags said.

Then Brooklyn returned and collected the used teacups. "Did you enjoy the tea?" she asked.

"Delicious and refreshing as usual," Saddlebags replied, "kind of like looking at you."

Brooklyn gave her father a blushing smile. "And you, darling?" she asked Riley.

"A little bitter at first, but it's growing on me."

"He'll be a pup yet," Saddlebags stated puffing out his chest. "A natural born charmer, quite like myself."

Brooklyn shook her head and smiled. "You should have seen him when he first asked me out." Brooklyn shot us a mischievous grin. "It took him eighty-seven seconds of moping before he realized I had said yes."

"You counted!" Saddlebags shot her with a wry smile.

"There was a very large clock nearby." Brooklyn's smile never left her face.

"Wait, you didn't know at first?" Riley asked quizzically.

Saddlebags smiled. "I took a chance thinking no way a girl like that would say yes. So, when she did, it took me a minute."

"And almost a half," Brooklyn said matter-of-factly.

"The important thing is," Saddlebags said, "I asked, and she said yes."

Saddlebags patted the young boy on the shoulder. "I think it's time you headed back."

"Will I be able to return here?" Riley's eyes pleaded.

"I look forward to it," Saddlebags stated. "It's been so long since I've been able to read the Saddlebag Chronicles to anyone. I'd hate to lose a curious mind and a grateful heart like yours."

Riley gave him a sad, longing smile. "I can't wait for the next one."

"Come, darling," Brooklyn beckoned him. "It's time to get you home."

Riley followed the matronly vixen, taking every opportunity to drink in the wondrous place around him. As they neared the exit, Riley felt as if it were his last chance to ask anything.

"Have you ever been to Brooklyn?" Riley asked, feeling dumb that his first question was so immature.

"My mom and I were born there," Brooklyn replied.

Riley's eyes went wide. "You were?"

"Well, my mother wasn't actually born, so much as began to exist," Brooklyn explained. "My mother came into being once the New York Public Library began to turn from an idea into a reality. She said there were only three of them when it first started."

Riley held back a gasp, "The New York Public Library is a haven house?"

"It is a gateway to a haven house, considered one of the biggest, if not the biggest in the world and housing everything the world knows and quite a few things it doesn't."

Riley knew he must have been gawking, "How many spirits are there?"

"Hundreds, the last I checked, probably thousands by now," Brooklyn replied. "Once the library was up and running, spirits from all over the world came to share and exchange knowledge." Brooklyn's smile grew wider. "That's how my mom met my dad."

Riley could tell she wanted to tell that story, and luckily for her, he desperately wanted to know.

"What happened?" Riley asked, not bothering to hide the stars from his eyes.

"My father was a spirit at Oxford University, a true gentleman who had spent his youth in the Irish countryside. He was the spirit that brought the original Alice in Wonderland to the New York Public Library, and my mother was the first spirit he showed it to."

"Wow!" Riley was awestruck.

"Indeed," Brooklyn replied.

"Later, my father took my mother to the rolling Irish hills that had sung and carried all Irish folklore to the four corners of the earth. St. Patrick himself preached on them."

"The air," she breathed in as if remembering, "fills your hearts as well as your lungs, and puts a song that never goes away right here," she tapped Riley's chest and gave him a smile as bright as Riley had ever. "My parents danced and sang together, ran and played like young foxlings before collapsing in a big heap at the bottom of a shady hill." Brooklyn shook her head and smiled, "My dad still says he could hear the hills and angels sing when he kissed my mom."

"Sounds magical," Riley said, grinning like a Cheshire cat.

"It was," Brooklyn said with a wink, "That's why I brought Saddlebags to the same spot."

"You didn't!" Riley gasped, the smile still plastered to his face.

"I did," Brooklyn shook her head. "When he first breathed in that Irish air, he couldn't stop howling."

Riley looked dumbstruck at the idea of Saddlebags howling. He wouldn't know he had it in him.

"He began chasing me, singing and beckoning me to fall into his arms. I ran caroling and coaxing him to come to me," Brooklyn clutched her blouse. "My heart was beating out of my chest the entire time. When he finally caught me, we both burst out laughing and fell at the bottom of some shady hill." Brooklyn got a far-off look in her eye. "I still think it was the same one."

Brooklyn hugged herself, "I can still feel the pillow-soft grass under us, his arms wrapped around me, and I never wanted to leave."

"Could I become like you and Saddlebags?" Riley asked from the depths of his heart.

"Maybe," Brooklyn frowned. "I wouldn't know how you would go about the process or if the knowledge to do so even exists."

Riley looked as disappointed as he felt. Brooklyn placed a paw on his shoulder.

"But hey," she said, her smile returning, "anything's possible."

As Riley made his way towards the gateway, he heard Brooklyn mutter, "Be still my beating heart." He turned around to see Saddlebags slowly wrap his arms around her before pulling her into a hug and nuzzling her neck. Brooklyn let out a deep, loud chuckle as she returned his affection. Before he crossed the threshold, Riley smiled to himself as he began to wonder when he might be seeing a newborn foxling.

Discussion Questions

1. What's the best part of Saddlebag's library?
2. What do you think is the best part of the festival?
3. What food would you like to try?
4. How long do you think you could dance?
5. Why is Estella scared? When does she start to gain courage?
6. Why is Ridley depressed? How does he resolve it?
7. Why is Estella depressed? How does she resolve it?
8. Do you think there's a Heaven?
9. Can you believe there's a Heaven if you don't believe there's a Hell?
10. Are love and life preplanned or random? Why do you think so?
11. What would you do if you were a fox on the final night of the festival?
12. If you have been in a position like that one, what did you do?
13. What did you learn from the book? What would you like to learn next?
14. Riley's a boy. Why did he need to hear a romance?

ABOUT THE AUTHOR

Brock Hunt is an up-and-coming writer from Paragould, Arkansas. His first book, *Enter the Cat Cings Court*, is available on Amazon. The *Saddlebag Chronicles* Cinder Rabbit is his second book and longtime passion project. Brock has a Chemistry degree from the University of Colorado Denver. Brock enjoys reading, long walks, weightlifting, Bible study, cooking, books and movies of all genres and stories of all kinds. Brock encourages everybody to read all the books they can, and anyone who wants to write to start and never stop.